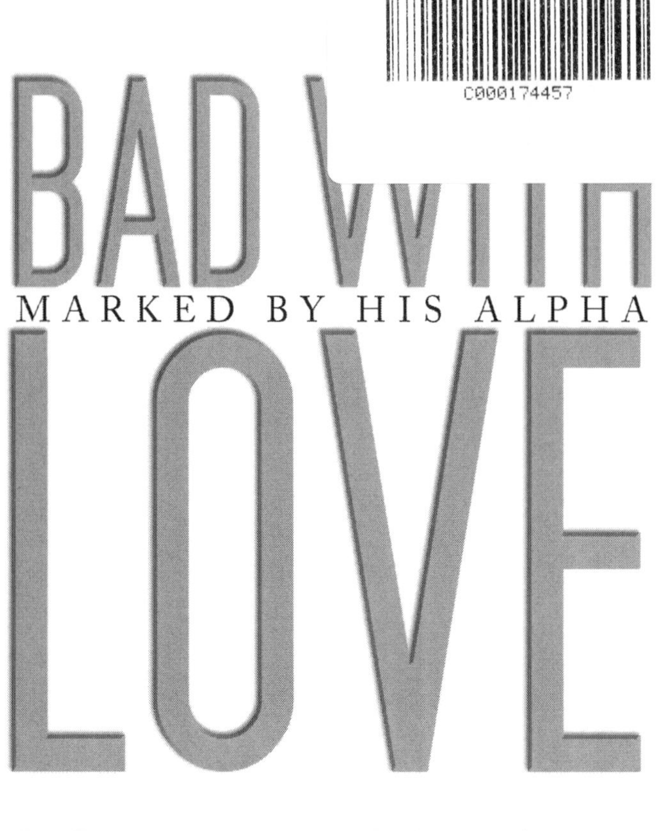

C000174457

MARKED BY HIS ALPHA

SOPHIE O'DARE

AN
ALPHA/BETA/OMEGA
STORY

LITERARY SERVICES

ALSO BY SOPHIE O'DARE

Marked by His Alpha

Bad With Love

Maybe Tomorrow

Omega on the Run

Desperate to Marry

Leading Love

Focused on Him

Taking Two

Faking for Real

Taming His Alpha

Tails x Horns

You to Me

Just Not You

As You Are

Kiss Me Please *(novella)*

Heat Me Up *(novella)*

Play With Me

Sweet Blood

First Bite

For future Sophie O'Dare releases, keep an eye on:

www.SophieODare.com

BAD WITH LOVE © copyright 2021 Sophie O'Dare

All rights reserved. No part of this publication may be reproduced, distributed, or transmitted in any form or by any means, including photocopying, recording, or other electronic or mechanical methods, without the prior written permission of the writer, except in the case of brief quotations embodied in critical reviews and certain other noncommercial uses permitted by copyright law.

This is a work of fiction. Names, characters, businesses, places, events and incidents are either the products of the author's imagination or used in a fictitious manner. Any resemblance to actual persons, living or dead, or actual events is purely coincidental.

Cover Design Copyright © 2021 L&L Literary Services, LLC

Book Design Copyright © 2021 L&L Literary Services, LLC

www.llliteraryservices.com

Copy Editing by L&L Literary Services, LLC

Printed in the United States of America.

ISBN: 978-1-953437-39-6

First Printing, 2021

SYNOPSIS

An Alpha who gets under his skin. A family that demands too much. A night that changes everything.

Warren Heardst has never been lucky. He spent his entire life in competition with his high school nemesis, Roman Markham, who has always been better in school, better in sports, and better in love.

Working hard, Warren builds a life outside of his overbearing family, but he can't seem to escape Roman. The other man is always there, pushing Warren to prove he can be successful. But on the cusp of realizing his goal, a family emergency rears up to ruin everything.

Suddenly, his dream is being ripped away. With a marriage contract on the table, will Warren lose his chance at happiness? Or will his bad luck with love lead him unexpectedly into his rival's arms?

THE ALPHA/BETA/OMEGA WORLD

Alpha: Can be male or female. Naturally charismatic with a dominant personality, so they tend to be in positions of power. Can use Command to enforce their will on weaker Alphas and Omegas who are not protected by an Alpha. When near an Omega in Heat, Alpha's are driven to protect and mate with the Omega.

Beta: Can be male or female. Regular citizens without any atypical behavioral traits. Are not affected by an Alpha's Command or an Omega's Heat.

Omega: Can be male or female, and both genders are capable of becoming pregnant during their

Heat. Omegas, up until recently, have struggled to hold onto regular jobs due to going into Heat every month. During Heat, they release a pheromone that attracts Alphas. The pheromone can now be suppressed through the use of suppressants.

Suppressants: Medication Omegas take to help suppress their pheromones during their monthly Heat.

Heat: A three day period every month in which Omegas release a pheromone to attract an Alpha and are overwhelmed with the need to mate. The effects can be reduced by the use of suppressants.

Command: An Alpha's ability to enforce their will on weaker Alphas and on Omegas. Betas are not affected by an Alpha's command.

Mark: During Heat, an Alpha is driven to Mark their partner by biting the back of their neck. The Mark stays in place for a month, claiming the breeding right of the Marked Omega. It also stops other Alphas from Commanding the Marked

Omega. If the same Alpha Marks an Omega three times, it becomes permanent. If the Alpha does not Mark the Omega, the Mark fades after their next Heat, leaving them available for other Alphas.

1

The spice of cinnamon, cardamom, and black tea fill the air as I open the large drum in the storeroom and shovel loose tea leaves into the smaller, customer-friendly jars we keep on display up front. With fall setting in, chai lattes are back on the rise, and I make a note to order another barrel. At the rate we're selling this blend, we'll be out before the apple harvest blend kicks in.

After five years of running my boutique tea shop in the heart of Rockhaven's historic district, we've finally gotten out of the red financially. Through hard work and creative advertising, we've built a solid, passionate customer base, stabilized the menu, and even opened an online shop to ship our teas around the world.

For the first time in my life, I feel like my dream can be a reality. With the shop's current income, I'll be able to pay back the loan I took out from my family in another five years, seven if I hire some much-needed assistance, and then this store will truly be mine.

The quiet of the backroom gives way to the buzz of conversation as I return to the front of the shop and slide the jar of tea onto the cherry oak shelf alongside the other black teas.

"Warren, we'll need more snicker-doodle cookies soon," Mia calls from the brewing station. "Better make some apricot crisps, too."

"Got it!" Shifting the jar on the left to even out the spacing, I pop into the small kitchen and load a tray with cookies from the freezer.

To cut down on cost, I make them at home and bring them into the shop, along with the other pastries and desserts we sell. Eventually, I'd like to outsource this part of the business, but it's not in the budget. Yet.

I set the timer on my phone and shove it into my back pocket so I'll feel the buzz, then return to the front just as the bell above the door jingles a merry welcome.

Automatically, I turn a smile on our new customer

that turns brittle and forced when I recognize the tall man who takes a seat at a two-person table near the window.

The cool, fall sunlight perfectly highlights his strong jawline and the russet hues in his auburn hair. Roman Markham. Alpha asshole and my high school nemesis. We'd been in every class together at the prestigious private school our wealthy parents shipped us off to and been in competition with each other since day one. He always scored a few points better on tests, won first place in every sport, and ruthlessly stole every boyfriend I had only to dump them a week later.

I thought I escaped him when we attended different universities, but the day after we officially opened the tea shop, he showed up with his critical gaze, pointed out the places we needed to improve to reach a client base willing to pay ten dollars for 'weeds in water', and swept out. He returned a month later, pleased to see we made the changes he suggested—changes that had already been on my list after our soft opening—and has come here every day since, when he's not out of town.

I would ban him if he didn't bring his rich friends with him sometimes, friends who return to buy our custom tea blends and leave the store carrying bags with our logo on them, promoting us to their other rich friends.

If not for Roman's patronage, we might still be in the red, and it bothers me to no end that I'll never know how much of my current success can be laid at the feet of his polished loafers.

Mia hustles up to me, a cup of tea in one hand and a plate with two almond biscotti in the other. Pink flushes her cheeks as she glances at Roman. "Can you take his service today? My Heat is coming in a couple days and…"

I drag in a deep breath and force down the disappointment when I can't smell an increase in her pheromones. As an Alpha, I should be able to sense an Omega's Heat, even a few days out, but all I smell is tea and the baking snicker-doodle cookies.

My brows pinch with concern as I take the tea and cookies from her. "Do you need to go home early? I can cover your shift."

"No, I have my suppressants, so as long as I stay behind the counter, I should be fine." She gives me an impish smile. "You can't use me as an excuse to duck out of your family dinner tonight."

I widen my eyes at her in mock affront. "I would *never*."

"As soon as Steve gets here, you're gone, mister."

Gently, she pushes me toward the end of the counter. "And don't get caught up chatting and forget you're baking cookies."

A flush creeps up my cheeks. That only happened once, and only because Roman was being particularly nitpicky that day. It's not like I go out of my way to talk to him.

With a deep breath, I straighten my spine and head for Roman's table, my best customer service smile in place.

Three steps away from him, Roman's cool blue eyes lift from the tablet in his hand and meet mine unerringly, as if he knew I would be the one to come to his table.

My gut tightens uncomfortably, but I refuse to give him the satisfaction of looking away first. This is *my* business, a shop I built from the ground up, the one place in life where I have full control, and I won't let him intimidate me here.

Smile still in place, I set his tea and cookies on the table in front of him. "If you'd like a refill, just let me know, and I'll bring it out."

He pulls the tea closer with one long, elegant finger. "Earl Grey with honey?"

I can smell the sweet, citrus bergamot from where I stand. It mingles perfectly with the clean scent of his expensive cologne. "Yes, your usual. Did you want something new?"

"No, this is perfect." He lifts the cup to his lips and breathes in the steam. "Your shop has the best in town."

"The best 'weeds in water' in town," I say, unable to keep the snap from my voice.

The corners of his mouth twitch. "Indeed."

I turn on my heel, ready to leave, when he catches my wrist.

Goose bumps rise all over my body, and I instinctively yank my arm away as I turn back, my brows lifted. "Did you need something else?"

"Why don't you sit? Take a break?" He gestures to the chair across from him. "We haven't caught up in a while."

"What's there to catch up on?" I glance around at the other customers. "I have work to do."

"You always have work." He turns in his seat, draping one arm over the back of the chair. "Surely you can afford to take a break every so often."

I stiffen at the criticism. "Not all of us have jobs handed to us by our parents."

A muscle in his jaw jumps. "No, just stores bought by them."

Anger shoots through me, but I can't refute the statement. Not yet, anyway.

My pocket buzzes, saving me from saying something I'll regret, and I stomp away from Roman without another word.

Once I officially own this place, the first thing I'll do is ban Roman Markham from ever stepping foot in here again.

The man has a skill for burrowing beneath my skin, and I can't wait until he's out of my life for good.

2

Uneasiness rolls in my stomach as I follow the butler to the dining room.

Since I moved out to boarding school, then university, I hadn't felt as comfortable in the family home. It has too much space, too much opulence, for four people and their staff. Two now, since dad skipped out and I decided to rent my own place after graduating. I mean, who needs two ballrooms in this day and age? Or a living room that can fit a two-story tall Christmas tree and a hundred guests comfortably? Half the mansion is closed off year-round, and more servants than family live here.

My shoes echo on new, white marble flooring with veins of gold running throughout. Mother had it installed when my father abandoned the family to run away with his secretary. Everyone had known of their affair for years now—my parent's marriage had always been about business, not passion—but it came as a shock when he gave up the family fortune for love. I was the only one who didn't resent him for choosing his heart over the cold sterility of this house. I just wished he'd call every so often.

The butler stops at the door to the dining room. "Master Warren has arrived, ma'am."

"About time." My mother sets down her wine glass to stand. "We were beginning to worry you weren't coming."

Considering I'm five minutes early, that's a bit melodramatic. But my family always worked under the philosophy that punctuality equaled tardiness.

I walk past the butler and over to my mother, dropping a kiss to the air over her powdered cheek before I set a small gift bag on the table beside her chair. "Mother, you look stunning, as always."

It's not a lie, though I'd say it regardless. My mother has always taken pride in her appearance and it shows in her flawless complexion, which she highlights with a light dusting of makeup, and in her slender, athletic figure wrapped in a blue silk business suit that perfectly brings out the inky highlights in her raven dark hair. At nearing sixty, she outshines many of the debutants I've encountered over the years.

My sister mirrors her in every way, from her sleek black hair to her slightly more form-fitted suit. And if I looked in a mirror, I'd have to admit I'm a male version of her with shorter hair. Genetics runs strong in our family.

Circling the table, I drop a kiss near my sister's cheek as well and deposit her gift on the table. "Good to see you, Katheryn."

"I wish I could say the same." She wrinkles her nose as she takes in my humble brown corduroys and the cream polo I wore to work today. "Have you forgotten how to dress for dinner?"

"Come now, dear, you know he's diligent with his little hobby." Mother plucks at the tissue paper that holds her gift. "What have you brought us today? Another sample from your shop?"

I fight down the irritation at my tea shop being downsized to a hobby. After five years and weeks of working without taking days off, I had hoped she'd finally realize I'm serious about what I do. But when you're born into excess, I guess everything you do is a hobby. It's not like I *need* the shop. I have a trust that matures when I turn thirty, only two years away, and all I've ever had to do is ask for something to have it be delivered.

That's part of why I work so hard at the tea shop to make it a success. I want to know that what I have in life is *mine* and not an extension of my family.

I take my seat on my mother's right as she pulls out a small bag of cinnamon and orange-infused black tea. It's one I've been working on all summer and hope to launch it in time for Christmas.

She sniffs the bag delicately before holding it out to the butler. "Archibald, please make us a pot to try. My son's teas are always a delight."

"Right away, ma'am." He takes the bag and strides for the doorway to the kitchen.

"You know his name is Stirling, right?" I say once he's out of earshot.

My mother shrugs. "I can't be bothered to memorize a new name every time there's a change in staff."

Which is exactly why the staff here changes so often. Every new employee signs an NDA before they're hired so they can't tell outsiders how horrible my family is to work for.

Katheryn moves her gift off to the side without opening it, which I expected and why I gave her peppermint sugar scrub instead of tea. She'll likely re-gift it without ever opening it, so I hope whoever receives it appreciates my efforts.

Mia had suggested a spa line for the website, an idea I'm still playing with. Sugar scrubs are easy to make and store, but would people go to a tea shop to buy them? They're edible, at least, in case anyone mistakes them for a tea additive.

I pluck the white cloth napkin from my stack of plates and settle it on my lap before I turn to my mother. "So, to what do we owe this family dinner?"

The last time we had one was when Mother informed us Father would no longer be coming home. The time before that had been when Nana Rose passed away, leaving her fortune to her other daughter, much to my mother's rage. But Aunt Theona is younger by two decades and has five Alpha children to raise, while Katheryn and I were both already through schooling by that point.

Mother lifts her glass of wine and takes a dainty sip before setting it down. "Must we get right to business? It's been so long since you've both been at the family home. You, with your little shop, and Katheryn with her flat in the city. My nest is empty."

I'd hardly call Katheryn's place little. She rents the penthouse suite in the heart of Rockhaven's party scene, within walking distance of any form of high-class entertainment. But she still spends most weeks here at the mansion. Mother just misses that while she's out doing charity work to support underprivileged ballerinas, or whatever her newest cause is.

"The shop's busy," I say as she takes another sip of wine. "You should stop in to see it."

"Oh, no, I simply don't have the time." Mother blots non-existent drops from her perfect, smudge-resistant lipstick. "Between luncheons and budget meetings, my entire day is gone."

Katheryn nods in agreement, as if it's perfectly acceptable that neither of them has made it to my store since it opened. Father was the only one who showed any interest when he helped me scout locations and research tea vendors. But now he's too busy with his new wife to drop by, either.

The butler returns, a silver teapot and china cups balanced on a tray. Behind him follows the house chef with a platter of tiny triangle sandwiches and cups of soup.

Not the elaborate meal I expected when I arrived. Is Mother back on one of her diets? I'll have to grab a burger on my way home. There's no way I'll fill up on what looks like tomato and prosciutto sandwiches with gazpacho.

"Thank you, Archibold," Mother says as the food is placed in front of us and he pours the tea. "I will call if you're needed again. Otherwise, please make sure we are not disturbed."

"Yes, ma'am." With a bow, he ushers the chef back to the kitchen.

As they leave, the knot in my stomach returns. This feels like Father's leaving all over again. But what new catastrophe could have struck the family?

I force myself to take a spoonful of gazpacho, not tasting the hearty blend of vegetables or the tang of lime and vinegar. The quiet clink of silverware against bowls fills the room, no one making conversation. We don't have much to talk about in general, and tension fills the space, making it even more uncomfortable. It feels like a pendulum swings over our heads, waiting for the end of dinner before it comes crashing down.

When Mother pushes her bowl and plate of untouched sandwiches aside, Katheryn and I do the same with a sigh of relief.

Mother picks up her teacup and takes a sip before pushing that aside as well. "I have news, my darlings, and it isn't good."

The knot in my stomach tries to push out the small amount of food I forced down.

Katheryn bypasses her teacup and goes straight for

her wine glass, clutching the slender stem for support. "Is Father coming back?"

For a moment, Mother looks startled, as if the idea had never occurred to her. And why would it? She got what she wanted from the marriage. A higher station within society, numerous properties, and children to continue the family line.

At last, she shakes her head. "No, darling. Gregory has left the country."

It takes me a second to place the name. "Our accountant?"

She nods sharply. "Yes."

Kathryn relaxes. "Well, that's unfortunate, but hardly worthy of calling us home to make the announcement. I'm sure one of the partners—"

"He's taken our fortune with him," Mother cuts in.

"What?" Katheryn shrieks, while the tension in my body seeps away. "How could he?"

"He had unlimited access to our accounts and invested in several offshore businesses, which he now controls." Mother gives us a solemn stare. "We are now destitute."

As Katheryn sputters, I fight back a laugh. "We're hardly destitute. We can sell some properties, cut back on expenses…"

I trail off as Mother shakes her head. "No, darling, you are not grasping the situation. The life we lead takes funding. Funding that's now *gone*. Yes, we can sell a few of our properties, but that will take time, and the longer we go without, the farther we fall in society."

"Katheryn giving up the penthouse in Rockhaven will save eleven-thousand a month. More without having to pay for all those parking spots for the cars she never drives," I reason, and my sister turns red with fury. "There's the Bentley in the garage that I never accepted. It can also be sold." I glance around the expensive dining room with the three crystal chandeliers and the silk wallpaper. "You can move to one of the vacation homes and sell this place for a few million."

"Stop." Mother holds up a hand. "We are the Heardst Family Alphas, and we will *not* be selling off our estates just because some middle-management stooge stole from us. We have a position to uphold in society. People look up to us to set an example. We weathered your father leaving us because our name meant more than the scandal, but if this gets out, everyone will turn their backs on us."

I shake my head. "But, if we're broke…"

"As you said, we have options." She reaches out

and cradles the teacup in her hands. "First, you will move back to the family house. We will sell the tea shop to get us through the next few months."

"Excuse me?" The blood drains from my face, leaving me light-headed. "That's my business."

"It's our family's investment, and one that has drained enough of our funds," she says coolly.

"But it's turning a profit!" I protest. "It pays for all of my expenses now, my apartment, my groceries, my car—"

"Yes, your car." Her lip curls in disgust. She's never approved of my choice to drive a modest four-door sedan over the expensive car she bought me for my twenty-fifth birthday. "It's time you stop playing at working for a living, darling. It's fun to spread your wings a little, but the family needs you now. Both you and Katheryn are at the age to marry, and I've already made arrangements with suitable matches."

"As long as I get to keep the penthouse, I don't care who I marry," Katheryn snaps. "But if they expect more than two children, I'll need monthly bonuses. And I want a full staff of nannies."

As Mother nods in agreement, I stare at my sister in shock. How can she be so ruthless? A penthouse isn't worth selling your life.

"I'll have our lawyers put it in the marriage

contract. The man I've selected for you comes from a good Alpha family, guaranteeing our line will carry on. I have someone of means selected for Warren. A young man who will easily rebuild our family fortune." She turns to me and *tsks* loudly. "Don't look so horrified, Warren. You always knew you'd be expected to marry for the family. You'll get along with your new husband. You've actually already met."

My lips feel numb as I ask, "Who?"

"Young Herold Freely. He just turned twenty." She lifts her cup to her lips without drinking. "You remember him, don't you? You met at last year's Christmas party."

"The banker's son?" I shake my head in denial. This can't be happening. "He's barely legal."

"But legal he is." She sets her cup down with a click. "You should be thankful. It's not easy to find a male Omega who comes with enough money to buy our family name. If not for him, you'd have to accept a female, which I know you would struggle with."

Struggle with. As if being gay is an inconvenience I can just set aside. "I won't do it. You can't make me."

She arches one perfectly plucked eyebrow. "Stop being so childish. This is an honor, Warren. And a duty to your family."

"I don't need this mansion, though. Or our family

name. My shop can support me just fine." I push my chair back from the table. "I'm sorry this happened, but I won't be sold so you can keep living to your ridiculous standards!"

"*Sit down.*" The quiet Command knocks my knees out from under me, the weight of her Alpha control taking away my ability to move.

Even Katheryn whimpers and ducks her head.

I struggle against the need to obey, but I've never been a strong Alpha—I've never even Commanded someone—and my muscles shake with the effort before I sag in defeat.

"Now, then," she says as if she didn't just subjugate her own children. "I've already arranged to put the *family's* shop up for sale, and I've informed your apartment manager that you will be vacating the premise at the end of the month."

My mind scrambles for alternatives even as my body forces me to nod.

"And before you think about refusing your obligations, consider where you'll be if you fight this." She folds her hands on the table and leans forward. "Your shop *will* be sold, your apartment *will* kick you out. Your bank account, however paltry it is, belongs to the family. Your trust fund is gone. You have *nothing* if you leave here. You will be homeless and without a job. You will be on your own, begging your friends for a place to sleep, and how many of them will support you once they learn you are no longer a Heardst?"

My knees shake, and though the weight of her Command no longer holds me down, I can't force myself to stand.

She smiles in a perfect curve of red lips. "Now, let's have dessert while I tell you about your betrothed."

3

"Do you have any snicker-doodles?" the customer in front of me asks.

Shaking myself out of the stupor I've walked around in all day, I offer her a tired smile. "I'm sorry, we're all out for the day. Would you like a chocolate chip instead?"

When I arrived home last night, I wasn't in the right mindset to make a fresh batch of cookies. I'd fallen straight into bed and stared at my alarm clock until it buzzed for me to get up the next morning.

From the tea station, Steve gives me a concerned look as I prep the customer's order and direct her down the counter to wait for her beverage. If Mia hadn't already asked for the next three days off for her Heat, I would have called in sick today. Being here, in the place I love, knowing it will be torn down and made into something different, hurts too much to bear.

All night, my mind shuffled through different options on how I could save my dreams and my freedom. But even if I could come up with a business loan in time to buy the place, Mother would never sell it to me, and I can't spend the next five years rebuilding in a different location. I can't afford to pay back a loan, either. The current income just covers expenses and my living, with a small amount set aside for savings. Yes, my business projections said that would only improve, but not with adding a bank loan and starting over in a less ideal location.

And those friends Mother mocked me about? They don't even exist. Sure, I had my fair share in school, but they hadn't understood my desire to work while they traveled the globe on their family's dime. We'd drifted apart and fallen out of contact.

Mia would probably let me sleep on her couch for a few nights, but an Alpha in an Omega's house is dangerous when they have their Heat, even an Alpha who can't smell an Omega's pheromones, like me.

I've heard stories about the drive to mate, the overwhelming need that the Heat brings. And as much as I like Mia, I don't want her jumping me because she can't control herself.

Betas, like Steve, have it easy. They aren't driven by the same primal urges, nor are they subjected to an Alpha's will. Command slides over them just as easily as an Omega's pheromones.

If not for how readily I submit to an Alpha's Command, I would have labeled myself a Beta long ago. It would have brought shame to our family, who has bred Alpha's for the last five generations, but at least I would have been allowed to live my life free. No one is going to pay a huge dowry to marry a Beta.

Steve sets the to-go cup on the high bar and walks over. "It's my break time, but if you need me to stay on the floor…"

"No, go take your break." I force a smile that strains my cheeks. "I can handle the shop for fifteen minutes."

Behind his gold-framed glasses, his eyes pinch in concern. "Are you okay? You look pale. Are you feeling sick?"

Now that he mentions it, I do feel sick. And a little warm. But I shake my head. "I just had a hard time sleeping last night."

The worry doesn't leave his face. "Want me to brew you a cup of tea before I go?"

My smile gentles into something more genuine. "No, I'll make one for myself. We're slow today."

"Okay, if you're sure." He heads for the door to the back. "I'll be in the break room, so if you need me, I can come back out."

I wave him away and go to brew a cup of black tea. I should probably eat something, too. The gazpacho from last night wore off before I even left the mansion, and I hadn't stopped for my planned burger on the way home. Caffeine on an empty stomach is never good, but the pastries in the display case make my stomach roll with nausea.

When the bell over the door jingles, I glance up and stifle a groan as Roman heads for his usual table. I don't have the mental capacity to deal with him today.

Quickly, I brew a cup of earl grey for him and use the tongs to pull two biscotti from the case, sliding them onto a plate. Removing the strainer from the cup, I set it aside, take his order to his table, and walk away before he can start up a conversation.

A minute later, though, he joins me at the counter, his teacup in hand.

I can't fight my frown. "Is there something wrong with your order?"

He studies my face. "Are you feeling okay?"

"I'm fine." I drag in a steadying breath and catch the smell of his cologne. It's stronger today, with a hint of spiciness that catches at the back of my throat and makes my gut clench around the sour ball in my stomach.

Brows sweeping together, he leans across the counter for a better look at my face. "Are you sure? You don't look well."

"Do you need something?" I snap.

"Honey."

Unwillingly, my eyes drop to his lips, watching as they shape the word, before my attention jerks up. "What did you say?"

He lifts his cup. "You forgot the honey."

"Oh, sorry." I reach for the cup and almost drop it when our fingers brush.

Steadying it, I walk back to the prep counter and drizzle in the sweetener, then stir the tea until it dissolves. I should have forced myself to sleep last night. The fuzziness in my head is taking a toll. I never mess up Roman's order. Why would I? He hasn't deviated from it in five years.

I take the cup back to the counter, set it down, and slide it across to him. "It's on the house. Sorry for the mistake."

"There's no need for that. Add it to my tab." His

eyes sweep over me again. "Do you have time later? I thought we should—"

I shake my head before he finishes. "I have a thing tonight."

The reminder makes me feel even sicker. I'm supposed to report to the Wellington Hotel tonight to officially meet my future fiancé at one of my mother's auctions. Maybe if I talk to him, he'll call the whole thing off. It's my only hope. But then Mother will just find someone else with money and the desire for a fancy name.

"Warren?" Roman's voice jolts me out of my thoughts. "When will you be done tonight? Can we grab something after? A late dinner, or coff—" He cuts off, chagrined, as he glances at the shop around him. "Or tea?"

My frown returns. Roman's never invited me out. What's with the sudden desire to reconnect? It's not like we were friends in high school. "I don't know when I'll be done. It's one of my mom's charity things."

"The Wellington Gala?" When my frown deepens, he shrugs. "My parents are going. We can talk there, I suppose."

But hadn't he just asked me to meet up? Did he want me to go to the charity with him? That doesn't make sense, though. Roman and I don't socialize outside of his visits to the shop for his morning tea.

Then, I realize Roman will be there to witness me being sold off like the family stud, and my stomach heaves.

Without a word, I turn and sprint for the back room, barely making it to the toilet before I vomit. Only tea and acid come up, and after a moment, my stomach settles once more.

When I push to my feet, Steve hovers in the doorway. "Okay, I know you're my boss, but I'm sending you home. We can't have you getting customers sick."

I don't think I'm sick, not really, it's just all the stress and lack of sleep catching up to me. But I nod in agreement. "If Roman's still at the counter, can you tell him his order is on the house? I'm going to go out the back."

"Okay, no problem." Steve pulls a handful of paper towels from the dispenser on the wall and passes them to me. "You should stay home tomorrow, too. Take some meds and get some sleep. I'll call in Jessica to help."

Jessica's our part-timer. She's always looking to pick up extra shifts.

I nod again. "Okay, sounds good. If you need anything…"

"Go." He flaps his hand toward the door. "Get some rest."

As he disappears, I run cold water over my face and neck, then glance at my reflection in the small mirror over the sink. My hazel eyes look a little glassy, my face pale outside of a red tinge to my cheeks. Maybe I *am* sick.

Wiping my face dry, I take off my apron and head out the back door where I park my car, praying I don't run into Roman tonight.

Because, sick or not, no excuse will get me out of this gala. Only a miracle will save me from this marriage.

"You're a business major, right?" Herold asks as he clings to my arm.

The kid zeroed in on me as soon as I stepped into the hotel ballroom and hasn't left my side since, much to my mother's delight.

He still looks twelve, despite reassurances he just turned twenty. Did I ever look that young? I don't think so. He has a softness about his face and body that begs for someone to swoop in and take care of him, but I don't feel anything, no matter how much he presses up against me. I've never been into small guys. Most of the ones I've dated have been Betas with muscular builds who can meet my eyes without having to look up. They didn't expect or seek me out for my Alphaness, either.

Something I'm sure Herold will find lacking in me the longer we're together, which just turns me off even more.

"That's not ideal, of course, but Daddy will teach you what you need to know before you take over the family business," he rambles on, not even requiring my input to keep the conversation going.

Which is good, because, seriously, who still calls their father *daddy* at his age? If he calls me that in the bedroom, I'll never get a hard-on. I take another look at his soft cheeks. Not that that's a possibility, anyway.

While he rattles on about the future I want no part in, I let my attention drift over the room.

The black-tie event pulled in the upper crust of society, and they drift around the room, bidding on the charity items displayed on tables pressed up against the wall. The bigger items will go up for auction after the dinner service, which is scheduled to start in an hour. For now, a string quartet plays on the stage, the soft lilt of violins slipping through the crowd.

Between all the people and Herold, I feel too hot in my suit jacket and tie, but I can't take them off until cocktail hour. Sweat slips down my spine, and my head still feels fuzzy, even after the three-hour nap I managed to take before coming here. I want to escape outside and cool off, but I don't see that happening any time soon.

My eyes land on the bar, and I look down at Herold. "Do you want anything to drink?"

His mouth snaps closed mid-word, and I belatedly realize he was still talking. Not that he'd stopped all night. His lips purse, and for a moment, I see the future we'll have together, filled with his endless nattering over things I don't care about interspersed with pouty displeasure if I step out of his box of expectations. Which, as he explained in detail, is Alpha arm candy that runs his family business for him while he pops out babies.

Yes, babies had already come up in conversation. He wants one a year until he's thirty, starting as soon as possible. He even hinted we could start tonight and slipped a key card into the inner pocket of my jacket.

Not happening, kiddo. Not tonight or any other night if I can figure out a way to escape this destiny.

After a long pause, he smiles prettily. "How about a cosmopolitan with cherries?"

"Sure." I nod to a nearby table. "If you want to sit, I'll be right back."

He walks his fingers up my chest then tugs playfully on my tie. "Don't keep me waiting, lover."

My dick doesn't even twitch with reactionary interest. This will never work.

As soon as he releases my arm, I spring across the room, eyes fixed on the bar. If I can't escape outside, I can at least get a drink to soften the torture of the night.

The room grows warmer the farther away from the entrance I walk until my face flushes from the heat. As I wait in line for the bar, I try to loosen my tie without undoing it. Does the place not have an air conditioner? Or can it just not keep up with the number of people packed in here?

Sweat drips down my temple, and I use my cuff to wipe it away.

"What can I get for you?"

Blinking, I look up and find myself already at the bar. I don't remember the line moving and quickly skim the bottles. "Um, virgin cosmopolitan with cherries and a shot of whiskey." I wipe my forehead again. "Do you have ice water back there?"

Nodding, the bartender grabs a pitcher and fills a tumbler with ice water before he makes the drinks I ordered. As I chug the water, I don't pay attention to what goes into the cosmopolitan, or how he makes a drink that's half vodka virgin. I don't care so long as Herold stays completely sober tonight. He's already too handsy for my taste. When the bartender slides the shot in front of me, I shoot it back, then grab the pitcher and refill my tumbler with more water.

The booze doesn't help the boil of heat under my skin, and I press the cold glass to my cheek as I take the cosmo and step away from the bar.

"Who's the kid?" a smokey voice murmurs into my ear, and goose bumps rise all over my body.

I recognize the cologne as quickly as I do the voice and keep walking.

"Are you ignoring me now?" Roman steps in front of me, forcing me to stop or run into him. "Who's the kid who keeps groping you?"

"Why, you want to steal him from me?" I gesture with the glass of water. "Take your best shot."

"So, you're not interested in him?" Something like relief flickers across his face before amusement replaces it, and anger sparks inside of me.

What, is it only worth stealing the guys I might *actually* like?

I lift my chin. "He's my intended."

The amusement vanishes in an instant. "Your intended for what?"

"Marriage."

When I move to step around him, Roman catches my arm to stop me. "You're not serious, are you?"

I look at him, meeting his eyes squarely. "Do I look like I'm joking?"

As he searches my face, his expression hardens. Before I can stop him, he slips his hand inside my jacket, fingers slipping over my chest. My pulse leaps at the light touch, my body reacting far more to his accidental brush than it has all night to Herold's groping. Roman's hand slips into my pocket, and he plucks out the key card my would-be fiancé slipped me earlier.

His eyes hold mine as he slips it into his pocket. "You don't mind if I take this, do you?"

I refuse to let his Alpha aura force me to look away. "Have I ever minded when you take what's mine?"

"I don't know. I can never tell with you." Reaching out, he straightens my tie. "This is the first time I've done it in a while. How does it make you feel?"

Relieved. Irritated. Trapped.

I lean forward, breathing in the citrus and spice of

his cologne. "He'll just give me another one. He's eager to start making babies. So, if you're going to make a move, you better do it fast."

Pale-blue eyes snap up to meet mine, and a low growl rumbles in his chest.

A thrill runs through me as I push past him, my blood buzzing with the high of finally getting one up on Roman Markham.

4

As the night wears on, Herold's clinginess and not-so-subtle innuendos grate on my nerves. It doesn't help that the heat in the room continues to grow, and I make so many trips to the bar to refill my water that I earn more than one pout from my date.

Does he think I'm trying to escape him? He's not wrong if he does. I feel sticky and uncomfortable with sweat, and my glass of water empties too fast to keep me cool.

Roman hovers on my periphery, but for all the openings I give him, he never takes his chance to swoop in and woo Herold away from me. The one time I want him to steal someone, and he chooses now to find a conscience.

After dinner, I escape to the bathroom, driven by a full bladder and a desperate need for a few minutes of silence.

Once I take care of the immediate problem, I linger at the sink, splashing cold water on my face and over the back of my neck. My face in the mirror looks flushed, my eyes glassier than they were earlier today, and I worry I really am coming down with a cold.

Taking tomorrow off is a good idea. Maybe I should see if I can take the day after off as well.

Last week, I never would have considered it. Rain or shine, healthy or sick, I was at the shop, even if it was just as support in the office. The tea store is my baby, my hopes and dreams. But now that my dream is being ripped away, I'm struggling to dredge up the determination to make sure it continues to succeed.

Behind me, a stall door opens, and a man stumbles out, his face red and his steps uneven. I passed him multiple times in line for the bar, and it looks like all those drinks finally caught up to him.

I turn off the water and grab a few of the paper towels from the neat stack in the basket. They're softer than the ones at my shop, cloth-like, and I feel guilty throwing them away after I pat my face dry.

Despite an entire row of options, the man stops at

the sink directly next to mine and eyes me in the mirror as he washes his hands.

His eyes slip down my body with interest. "You here for a hook-up?"

"No." I turn away.

For the second time in one day, a man grabs my arm to stop me from leaving. But unlike Roman, this guy doesn't try to be gentle as he pulls me closer. "Come on, you're obviously here looking for someone to take care of you tonight. Why not me?"

Booze washes over my face as he leans in close, and my skin crawls. "I'm not interested."

"What, you don't think I'm Alpha enough?" He yanks me closer, and my senses flood with his sour scent. "The stalls are nice and private here. *Come with me.*"

The Command shivers through me, and my foot inches forward before I stiffen my muscles. "What the hell, man?" Anger rushes through me, and I yank myself out of his grasp. "Did you seriously just try to Command me into fucking you? You think I won't report this?"

"Hey, I'm just trying to help you out here." His face flushes redder as he takes a step forward. "You come here like that, you're looking for this." He grabs his crotch in a crude gesture. "You shouldn't be so picky."

"Can't you understand when a guy says no?" Roman demands from behind me, and I spin to find him in the doorway, his eyes fixed on the guy accosting me. Fury fills his face, turning his blue eyes steely, as he Commands, "*Get out, and report your actions to security.*"

My knees tremble with the need to obey, and the Command isn't even directed at me. The drunk doesn't have a chance. Steps robotic, he marches out of the bathroom, leaving me alone with Roman.

We stare at each other for a few rapid beats of my heart before he storms forward and cups my face in his hands. "Did he hurt you?"

Unlike with the drunk, Roman's touch doesn't make my skin crawl. Far from it, in fact. The fire I had managed to quell with the cold water flares back to life, a furnace set to burn me alive. My already weak legs threaten to buckle with the sudden fever, and I reach for the counter to stop myself from sliding to the floor.

Roman's nostrils flare as he takes a deep breath. "Warren?" His thumbs sweep over my face. "Are you with me?"

I blink, my fuzzy head struggling to follow the

conversation. Of course, I'm with him. He's touching me, for God's sake, and my skin burns hotter with every second that passes.

I lick dry lips, my throat parched. "I think I'm sick."

"You're burning up." One hand moves to my forehead while the other slips beneath my collar at the back of my neck.

The tremble in my legs worsens, and I lift a hand to clutch his lapel. "I need to go home."

"You don't have that much time." He slips an arm around my waist. "Come on. I have a room upstairs. I'll get some medicine sent up."

"Why are you being nice?" I demand as he half carries me out of the bathroom. "Aren't you missing your opportunity to get with Herold?"

He snorts derisively. "I don't want that man-child."

"He's an Omega," I whisper as I lean more of my weight on Roman. "Rich family."

"So why are you interested in him?" He nods to a couple guests while shifting to block their view of me.

It's a level of consideration I never expected from him, and it makes me answer truthfully. "We're broke. My mother arranged it."

I feel his eyes on me as he stops at the elevator. "And that's the guy she chose for *you*?"

"Katheryn gets the prestigious spouse, I get the one willing to pay the most." A bitter laugh escapes me. "Marry for the family or get kicked out."

The elevator arrives, and he shifts me into the mirror-lined box, holding me close as he presses the button for the twelfth floor. "What about your tea shop? Surely that can support you?"

"Owned by my family. I was about to start paying it back next month; I had a five-year plan, but now it doesn't matter." Every breath I take fills my lungs with his cologne, and it makes thinking difficult. I groan against his neck. "Forget I said all this. I'm delirious. I'll go home as soon as I take some medicine."

"We'll see," he growls, and the vibration travels through my body, soothing some of the burn.

"That feels good." I press closer. "Do that again."

The rumble comes again as he cups the back of my neck. "You're going to be the death of me, Heardst."

"You can go back to hating me tomorrow," I moan into his neck. "For now, just keep talking."

He grips my neck tightens. "I don't hate you."

"Liar."

The elevator comes to a stop, and his hold on me shifts. "Can you walk? Or do I need to carry you?"

"We're almost the same size," I protest, though I don't want to peel myself off him. The burn in my skin feels better when we're close. "You can't carry me."

In response, he bends, one arm scooping behind my knees, and he hoists me off my feet with ease.

As he carries me from the elevator, my head falls back, and I groan. "Is there *anything* you're bad at?"

"Apparently, there's one thing I'm *very* bad at." He hoists me a little higher, and my head lands on his shoulder. "Hush. We're almost there."

When he stops talking, the rush of heat returns, crawling under my skin. His cologne makes it better and worse at the same time, both easing my fever and ratcheting it higher. "What brand do you wear?"

"What?" he asks, distracted as he stops in front of a door and tries to pull his key card from his pocket without dropping me.

"Your cologne." I loop my arms around his neck and snuggle in to drag the scent into my lungs. "What brand?"

"I don't wear cologne." He fumbles the card into the reader by feel and the lock pops open. "Why did you come tonight without taking your pills?"

Is he talking about cold medicine? I hadn't been sure I was sick when I left for the party. "I wasn't sure I needed them yet."

"Stupid risk to take," he mutters, dropping me onto the bed as if I'm burning him, and maybe I am. "You're lucky I came into the bathroom when I did."

"You're the stupid one." I tug at the tie around my neck, desperate to escape the noose. "I left Herold wide open for your advances all night, and you never took the bait."

"I already told you I wasn't interested in him." He pauses next to the phone to stare at me. "He wasn't the type of guy you usually go for, either."

I give up on getting my tie off, leaving it loose around my neck. "What kind of guy do I usually go for?"

"Taller, closer to your own size." He rakes a hand through his hair. "Auburn-haired and blue-eyed."

The way the lights in the room catch in the red strands of his hair distract me before the heat in my body reminds me of my original goal.

I go to work on the buttons of my shirt. "You're a liar. You were staring at Herold all night. Every time I glanced over, there you were."

"Sounds like you were the one staring." His eyes drift down my bared chest before he turns away and lifts the phone to his ear. A moment later, his low voice fills the room. "Yes, I need suppressants and candles sent to room 1215. As soon as possible."

Confused, I pause in the act of yanking my shirt from my pants. "Herold's not in Heat."

"They're not for Herold. I don't fucking care about your date tonight." Agitated, Roman hangs the phone up and rakes a hand through his hair again. "Would you stop undressing? I'm barely containing myself right now."

Frowning, I struggle out of my jacket. "Are *you* in Heat?"

"Are you mocking me? Is this some kind of elaborate joke?" He takes a jerky step toward the bed before he freezes. "Warren, *stop stripping*."

The Command rolls over me like a giant lick of heat, having the complete opposite effect on me from what he wants, and I fight the jacket off. It takes half my shirt with it, but the tie at my neck catches in the collar.

A knock sounds at the door, and Roman practically runs from the room to answer it.

He returns as I finally succeed in escaping the shirt, but it's not enough. My skin feels on fire, the fabric of my slacks chafing painfully, and I reach for my belt.

"Here, take the pills." Warren thrusts a bottle of water and a small paper cup at me.

I pause in my struggle with the belt to stare at the distinctive blue and red pills before I look back up at him. "Why are you giving me suppressants?"

He shoves the cup into my hand. "Because you're going into Heat."

"No, I'm not." I shove the cup back at him. "I'm an Alpha."

"No, you're not. You're an Omega." He draws in a deep breath, his pupils blown wide. "Your pheromones are so strong. If I hadn't lit the candle by the door, every Alpha in the hall would be smelling you right now."

I stare at him in shock. "I can't be an Omega. I'm almost thirty. I would have shown signs before now."

"Latent maturity." He licks his lips hungrily. "Likely brought on by stress." Then, he pauses. "This is your first Heat?"

"I'm not in Heat!" I say again, because he seems to have a hard time hearing my words right now. "Alphas don't have Heat."

Growling, he drops the pills as he lunges forward, catching the tie still around my neck to reel me in. His mouth slams over mine, his tongue thrusting past my surprised lips to stroke against mine.

My shock only lasts a moment before desire takes hold, and I kiss him back, my mouth hungry against his. He tastes like the bergamot-filled tea he drinks every morning with a hint of sweetness that makes me want to lick him all over and discover where else he's sweet.

When he pulls back, I whimper at the loss. I need his mouth back on mine, need the fullness of his tongue in my mouth.

He breathes heavily, his eyes locked on mine. "Tell me again you're an Alpha."

My lips part, but no words come out. I don't know what I am anymore. I've never felt like an Alpha, but I've never felt like an Omega, either. What I *do* know is what I *need* and lunge forward to seal our lips back together as I pull him down on top of me.

I don't like Roman Markham—he's been nothing but a thorn in my side since we first met—but as his hard body covers mine, I know he's the only one who can quench the fire that rages in my blood.

5

Roman's hands move all over my body, possessive and demanding as he learns my shape. My own hands dive beneath his suit jacket, digging into the hard muscles of his back and tracing the groove of his spine. He feels hot, too, like he's absorbing the fire that burns through me, and I lift my legs, hugging his hips with my knees, desperate for as much contact with his body as possible.

My dick strains against my zipper with a need I've never felt before, and I grind against his hard cock, any hint of embarrassment swept away by pleasure as he reciprocates with a skillful roll of his hips.

Whatever Roman feels toward me, he wants this, too, with a hunger that matches mine.

Reaching down, I grab his firm ass, urging him on, desperate for the release only he can give me.

He lifts off me far enough for his hands to slip between us and finds my nipples, plucking them between his fingers until my back arches. I've never considered myself a sensitive man, but everywhere he touches pulses with pleasure. His mouth leaves mine to trail hot, wet kisses down my throat and chest before he latches onto my nipple with his lips, sucking hard to pull it into his mouth. I moan and abandon my grip on his ass to fist his hair, not sure if I want him to continue or stop.

Growling, his teeth close over my nipple, and my hips jerk against him. He releases me, the flat of his tongue soothing the sting before he shifts lower, licking a hot line down my center. My straining dick nudges at his throat, then under his chin, demanding attention, and the rumble comes again, a low vibration against my dick before he drops past my waistband to mouth at my dick through the barrier of my slacks.

His hot breath and the light pressure of teeth against my head pull a moan from me, and I thrust toward his face, my hands in his hair demanding he take me in his mouth.

Taking the hint, he yanks my belt and pants open

before he hooks his fingers in my waistband, and I lift my hips, eager to be free of the restrictive fabric.

He makes quick work of my pants, stripping them off me along with my boxer briefs until I lay naked on the bed in front of him. My hard dick hugs tight to my stomach, precum leaking from the tip, and he smears his thumb through the fluid before lifting it to his mouth for a taste.

When he slips his thumb between his lip, my entire body shivers, my dick jumping for attention. Seeing those full lips wrapped around his thumb, tasting my cum, makes me imagine his mouth back at my dick, letting me sink into the heat of his mouth.

That low rumble comes from his chest again as he growls with approval before he reaches down and grasps my knees, spreading my legs apart so he can settle between them. The position leaves me open and exposed, not something I'm used to feeling, but with the fire that burns through me, a fire only he can ease, I don't care. I'll show him anything he wants if it means feeling his weight on me once more.

"Look at you." He runs his palms up my spread thighs, and the fire inside me burns hotter. "This is how you were meant to be. Spread out beneath me."

His words cut through the haze of lust that

muddles my thoughts, reminding me we're not lovers, we're not even friends.

"Take a good look," I spread my legs wider, reveling in the way his gaze focuses on my hard dick, in the way he licks his lips, hungry for another taste of my cum. I feel powerful right now, like I finally have the upper hand with this man, and can't help but taunt him. "You won't be seeing this again."

His heavy-lidded gaze drags up my body with the weight of a physical touch. "Now that your Heat has come, this will happen every month."

"We don't know this is Heat," I deny even as my body burns. "I could have been drugged."

In answer, he reaches between my legs, bypassing my straining dick and sensitive balls to slip his fingers into the crease of my ass. My hips jerk in response as he finds my entrance. With slick ease, he breaches me, and my ass clenches around his fingers, unfamiliar with the sensation of being filled.

I moan, hips rolling involuntarily, wanting something bigger and deeper. Eyes intent on me, he pushes more fingers into me, letting me ride them. My balls tingle, tension lacing through my muscles, and I whimper in protest when he pulls his fingers free, leaving me empty and wanting.

He lifts his hand to reveal his glistening fingers.

The sticky fluid coats my ass and thighs, too, something no Alpha would ever produce.

"You're an Omega," he says, pushing home the truth. He brings his fingers to his lips, licking away the fluid, and his eyes darken. "*My Omega.*"

I shiver as the Command rolls over me, imprinting his name into my flesh and carving it into my bones. Every part of my body cries *yes*, but I lock my teeth against speaking it. Speaking it makes this real, and that's just not an option. When this Heat fades, Roman will go back to being my nemesis, and I'll go back to hating him.

The reminder fades to the back of my mind, though, as Roman strips out of his suit jacket and shirt, revealing a body sculpted from years of sports and working out. Drool fills my mouth at all the hard ridges and deep valleys he reveals. No wonder he lifted me so easily in the elevator. All those muscles put my meager efforts to shame, but by the way he stares hungrily at me, he likes what he sees.

Slowly, he lowers the zipper on his slacks, and his hard cock springs free, the veins on his thick shaft forming ridges, and his tip red and glistening with pre-cum. Touching me excites him, and he stares at me as he fists himself, using his own cum to slicken his cock.

My ass clenches in response, my thighs growing stickier with my need. I've never let someone inside me. It's not something Alphas are supposed to do, and the size of his cock both scares and excites me. There's no question that he plans to take me, to imprint his body on mine, and I tremble with anticipation.

Smelling my excitement, his nostrils flare, and his self-restraint cracks. He grabs my waist, roughly yanking me farther down on the mattress before he pushes my knees up and out to expose my entrance. Then, his body covers mine, returning that delicious weight to press me into the mattress.

He grabs onto one of my arms, wrapping it around his back, and I eagerly pull him closer, my mouth on his throat as I drag his delicious scent into my lungs. When his cock nudges against me, all thoughts leave my mind except for the need to have him inside me.

Hot kisses pepper my face. "Open your eyes. Look at me."

Unsure when I closed them, I force my eyes open.

His face hovers over mine, his gaze intense. "Have you ever let someone do this before?"

He rubs against me for emphasis, taunting me without entering.

I moan, my body empty and desperate to be filled. "No."

"Good." He reaches between our bodies to grip my straining dick. "No one but me touches you from now on."

My mouth opens, maybe in agreement or maybe in protest, but he doesn't give me time to find out as he lines himself up and thrusts forward with a hard snap of his hips.

A moan of pleasure rips from my throat, and I clutch him tighter as sensation swamps me. It should hurt, I know it should hurt. There was little prep done, no real time spent stretching me for his invasion. But all I feel is pleasure as he pulls out, then drives forward, filling me with his hard cock.

The next time he pulls back, I clench around him, desperate to keep him deep inside.

Groaning, he fits my legs high around his waist. "That's it, learn my shape."

He sets up a steady, hard pace that has me moaning and writhing beneath him.

Sweat slicks our skin, and I lick the drops from Roman's throat before his head bends, and he captures my lips, his tongue thrusting in to lay claim to my mouth the same way his cock claims my body.

His hand on my dick pumps fast, and tension

builds in my body. My balls tingling, and I clamp down harder around Roman, trying to hold him inside me. I need that fullness, need—

He grinds into me, hips swiveling, and orgasm rips through me. My dick pulses in his tight grip, cum shooting over my stomach as my ass clenches and releases around his hard length.

He kisses me through the orgasm, his cock buried deep, until I begin to relax beneath him, my release leaving me light-headed. I've never experienced pleasure that intense before, or such a desperate need to be with someone. The fire that burned in my body now sits at a low simmer, eased for now, but ready to flare back to life at the slightest touch.

Mouth leaving mine, Roman eases out of my arms to sit back on his heels. His hands move to my hips, massaging my shaking muscles, before he grips me tight and slowly pulls from my body. His cock springs free, still hard and now glistening with my release. I stare at it, overwhelmed with how perfectly he fit inside my body, and the fever in my body boils to life once more.

It doesn't matter that I just came, that I shouldn't be able to get hard again so fast. Blood rushes back to my dick in a fever-hot streak.

Without a word, he rolls me onto my stomach

and parts my legs again. Instinctively, I push up onto my knees, following the direction of the hands on my hips until his hard cock nudges at my entrance. His hold on my hips tighten, and he yanks me back to slam into me once more, his hard thrusts shaking the bed.

I follow his direction, pushing back into his thrusts as I tilt my ass for a better angle. My hands flatten against the headboard, offering less give, so my body takes him deeper, and my moans fill the room, drowning out the slap of flesh against flesh and the wet sound of our bodies coming together.

The second time I come, he doesn't even stop, his thrusts drawing the orgasm out as my body desperately clutches at him.

When my legs give out after the third time, his weight covers my back, his cock a steady grind into my ass.

His smokey voice fills my ear with honeyed words. What he says gets lost in the fever haze, but my body understands, and I bow my head in acceptance.

He strokes down my side, one hand settling back on my hip while the other lifts to my neck, brushing the short black strands of hair aside to reveal my vulnerable nape.

"*My Omega*," he growls, sending a shiver through

me a moment before his teeth sink into my flesh, breaking skin to leave a lasting mark.

My final orgasm rips out of me on a scream of pleasure, my ass shoving up against him in demand, and his cock pulses, finally filling me with enough cum to extinguish the fire.

6

I wake sometime later, the fever burning beneath my skin once more.

After our first round of sex, I'd been too exhausted to move, and Roman had tucked me beneath the blankets and turned off the lights. With the blackout curtains pulled tight, only the faint flicker of the candle in the entryway lets off any light.

Lust clouds my thoughts again, and I roll over, reaching out, to find Roman already moving toward me, his body pressing me back into the mattress. Without the need for words, I curl my legs around his waist, my mouth seeking his in the semi-dark. There's less urgency this time when his hard cock slides into me, our bodies rocking together gently until I tense around him, my inner muscles pressing and releasing, and he stiffens, his cum filling me to ease away the fever.

We fall back to sleep still joined together, then wake to repeat the process.

When we're not sleeping, we're fucking, Roman always there and ready to ease the need in my body.

Time passes in a pleasure-filled haze of lust and desire, until the final time I wake and find my thoughts clear.

I blink the room into focus, my nose twitching at the medicinal scent of the candle that still burns in the hall. I vaguely remember Roman rising to light a new one a few times, usually returning with water that he coaxed me to drink before the fever took control once more, and I pulled him back into bed.

At the reminder, my entire body pulses with a dull pain that mostly centers on my hips and the back of my neck. I lift a hand, pressing on the ache as I trace the ring of teeth marks. Scabs scrape against my fingertips and realization dawns that Roman Marked me as his. I've heard stories of Alphas being overcome with the need to claim their partners, Marking them against all other Alphas. I'd never felt the need with my boyfriends, and now I know why.

I'm an Omega.

The knowledge shivers through me, my mind

struggling to accept this new status even after experiencing my first Heat. There hasn't been an Omega in the Heardst family line in over five generations. They pride themselves on breeding Alphas.

My gut clenches with trepidation. This news will change my mother's plans, but not in a good way. Obviously, I can't be expected to marry Herold, anymore. There's no advantage for my family for an Omega to marry another Omega. But me being able to breed… I can practically feel the dollar signs stamped on my ass now.

There aren't a lot of Omegas in upper-class society, and even fewer male Omegas. With an Omega's limitations at work, and an Alpha's natural charisma and power of Command, the wealthy tend to be Alpha heavy, which means marrying other Alphas or seeking Omegas outside of the upper-class.

As an Omega male from an upper-class family, Mother will have the pick of gay society in marrying me off. It won't even matter that we're broke. An Omega-Alpha marriage always results in Alpha or Omega children, with no risk of a Beta baby muddying the waters. The only thing that will slow her down is having to wait until after my next Heat before she can start interviewing potential spouses.

I press harder on the Mark on my neck. It will stay there until my next Heat as protection against other Alphas who might want to steal me away from Roman. But unless he Marks me again, it will fade, leaving me open for my pheromones to draw in a new partner. Three Marks and I'll be bonded to Roman for life.

My chest tightens at the thought, but I push away any feelings I have about that. What happened here doesn't change how we feel about each other, however tenderly he treated me. Roman won't Mark me again. He only did it this time because my pheromones pushed all his Alpha buttons.

I feel guilty about that, but really, how was I supposed to know? Omegas and Alphas usually mature at puberty, and that was half a lifetime ago for me. I need to see a doctor and find out why it took so long for my true nature to come through. And I need to get suppressants, so something like this never happens again.

The little blue and red pills are a godsend for Omegas, helping to reduce the effects of the pheromones they release as their Heat nears. Before they existed, rape was a huge issue in society, and Omegas often had a hard time getting jobs because no one wanted to risk an incident at the workplace.

As I remember the drunk in the bathroom, nausea rolls through me at what almost happened. Thank goodness Roman interceded when he did. He's not the complete asshole I always thought he was, and I feel bad I pulled him unwillingly into this issue. He could have just left me to my fate, but he stepped in and was swamped by my pheromones instead.

Shame adds to the guilt when I remember how he tried to resist, even requesting emergency suppressants be sent to his room. I was too stupid to take them, forcing him into using his body to ease my Heat.

God, how will I face him after forcing him to service me like some stud?

The bed shifts behind me and, panicked, I quickly shut my eyes, pretending to still be asleep.

A warm hand brushes against my forehead, then the back of my neck, and I will my pulse to stay steady, for my breathing to stay normal.

Is he checking if my fever returned? To see if he needs to let me use his cock again to ease my need?

His fingers linger on the Mark he left, gently tracing the rough circle.

Is he regretting that? Of course, he is. Why wouldn't he? He no more wants to bind himself to me than I want to be bound. At least it's only the first time. As long as we avoid each other going forward, it won't happen again.

After a moment, his touch falls away, and the mattress dips as he rolls back to his side, then stands and leaves the bed altogether.

I continue to feign sleep until the bathroom door shuts and the sound of the shower drifts out. Then, I scramble out of bed and find my clothes, yanking them on as I keep one eye on the bathroom door. My heart races, expecting Roman to pop out at any moment. I don't want to have that awkward morning-after conversation where he lets me down gently. I already know where I stand with him; I don't need to sit through him explaining it.

He was kind enough to stick with me during my first Heat; the least I can do is make things easier on both of us by staying out of his sight now. It won't be hard to avoid each other after today. The only time our paths cross is at my shop when he stops in for tea, and soon, that will be gone.

On my way to the door, I catch sight of a notepad on the small desk the room provides, and guilt swamps me once more. I'd be an asshole to not at least acknowledge how he helped me.

Pausing, I scribble out a quick note and set it next

to the cellphone Roman left on the table before I get the hell out of there.

Over the next week, I lose myself in work to keep my mind off the time I spent with Roman.

When I paid for the hotel room on my way out —another thank you to Roman for taking care of me—I'd been shocked to realize three days had passed since the charity auction. I arrived home to worried calls from my employees and a furious message from Mother about how I ditched Herold and ruined her careful plans. She was quick to inform me the tea shop had already been sold, and that I should pack my things and prepare to move back home.

She's already on the hunt for another rich fiancé for me, and I haven't worked up the nerve to tell her about my new Omega status.

I made it in to see a doctor and fill a prescription for suppressants. He had explained it was rare, but not unheard of, for an Omega to mature later in life, and how my firm belief that I was an Alpha probably helped to suppress my Heat. He also asked if I'd encountered a particularly strong Alpha who could have triggered the change, kind of my body's way of alerting me to the presence of a good mate.

When I admitted to going into Heat with Roman, and how we had a ton of unprotected sex, the doctor was quick to take a blood sample, which came back negative for pregnancy.

My relief had almost been enough to mask the twinge of disappointment the news brought. I told myself I didn't *want* to be pregnant, especially not with Roman's baby. No matter how much our time together filled my thoughts, he didn't want me for real. Everything that happened was driven by my new pheromones, and now that I have suppressants, that won't happen again. Not with Roman, and not with any other Alpha whose path I cross.

I pause in the act of loading cookies onto a tray to hook a finger under my new nape guard and pull it away from my throat. This is only the third day I've worn it, and the damn thing still feels like it's choking me. I purchased it at my doctor's recommendation as a precaution against future unplanned Markings. Not that I intend to fall into bed with anyone. I just have too much to figure out right now, and the nape guard removes one problem from my overwhelming list.

The door to the kitchen swishes open as Mia pops her head in, and I quickly pull my turtle neck up. I haven't told anyone about my new status, and the nape guard is a dead giveaway. I'm just glad we're heading into the cold season, where a turtle neck doesn't look out of place.

"Boss, You-Know-Who is here," she whispers.

Fixing my attention on the cookies, I nod in acknowledgment.

Her concerned gaze burns into my back, but she doesn't ask why I'm going to such lengths to ignore Roman. "I'll let you know when it's safe to come out."

I nod again and hear the door close once more.

I expected Roman to stop his morning visits after *The Incident*, but he keeps coming in like clockwork. At least his consistent schedule makes it easy to avoid being on the floor when he's here.

As I slide the tray of cookies into the oven, my pocket vibrates, and I close the oven door before digging it out. The display shows the house phone, and I almost decline, but I can't avoid my mother forever.

Sighing, I press the accept button and lift the phone to my ear. "Yes, Mother?"

Her brisk voice fills the line. "Oh, good, you answered."

I resist the urge to sigh again. She knows I'm at work right now, but she has the misguided opinion that, as the owner, I should be available whenever she needs me. "What can I do for you?"

"Your presence is required on Saturday for lunch. Katheryn's intended will be coming to the house, and I'd like all of the family to be there to meet him."

I close my eyes in frustration. "I'm working on Saturday."

"Then rearrange your schedule," she says sharply. "You owe me that much after how horribly you treated Herold. I had to send an apology gift to both him and his father, and you *know* we can't afford the extravagance in our current situation."

No, but she can somehow afford to continue to pay the exorbitant rent on Katheryn's penthouse and for the expensive luncheons she attends daily.

Sometimes, I wonder if I'm really her son, because I've never felt comfortable throwing money away with her level of abandon. Being adopted would certainly explain how I turned out to be an Omega. Too bad I'm her spitting image in male form. Her genetics completely obliterated my father's when it came to their children.

Knowing I won't escape this without a fight, I resign. "What time?"

"Two o'clock, sharp. Don't be late." The line falls

silent, and I pull the phone away from my head to find the screen now blank.

Apparently, social niceties are reserved for non-family members.

Pulling up my calendar app, I set myself a reminder.

Wouldn't want to be late to meet my future brother-in-law, after all. I just hope the poor guy can survive the combined force of my sister and mother better than I have.

7

Saturday arrives with a letter from the tea shop's new owner, informing me they'll be by on Monday to check out the space.

I don't recognize the business name on the letterhead and do a quick search on the internet, crossing my fingers that maybe it's a company that at least dabbles in tea. But the only thing the internet pulls up is a business license and location. They're local and too new for me to get my hopes up.

They're probably like I was five years ago, fresh from college and eager to put their stamp on the world by opening a small store. The likelihood they'll keep it as a tea shop is slim.

I open the store with a heavy heart. This weekend

might be our last, and I'll miss part of it because of my mother's stupid desire to pretend we're a united family.

At five to eight, I receive a desperate call from Steve, apologizing that his car broke down, and he'll be late. I try to ease his worry while, inside, I start to panic. Roman always stops in from eight-thirty to nine, and I've succeeded in avoiding that awkwardness so far. All I can hope for is a rush in customers that will keep me too busy to talk to him.

The rush in customers arrives, much to my relief, but Roman does not, and I find my eyes drifting to his usual table more than once, to see if I missed his entrance. In the past, when Roman planned to not visit, he always made some offhand comment about going out of town for a week. It had always felt like bragging at the time, but now I realize how much I've come to expect our brief interactions, and not having them now puts me on edge.

When Steve arrives at ten, I let him take over at the counter while I restock the pastry case.

In between customers, he joins me, his voice low. "I'm sorry I wasn't here this morning."

"It's no problem." I slide pastries to the back of the tray to load the fresh ones in front. "I can handle the place alone for a few hours."

His voice drops even lower. "Did You-Know-Who cause any problems?"

My lips twitch with an unwilling smile. "You guys can say his name. It won't hurt me."

Steve's eyes shift to the table Roman usually sits at. "Did he… Are you fighting? Or did he *do* something to you?" Then his eyes jump back to me, and he flushes. "Not that you have to say. It's just… Mia's been worried. If he bothers you, we can ban him from the shop."

Warmth fills me at their concern. "No, we didn't fight. Things are just complicated right now."

Steve's focus shifts to my throat, and his blush deepens. "You didn't use to wear… *that*." He taps the side of his neck in case I miss what he's talking about, and I tug my turtle neck a little higher. "We didn't know you were an Omega. We could have supported you better. We're friends, you know. You can rely on us more."

Eyes stinging, I look away as I blink back tears. I hadn't realized they thought of me like that. I mean, we get along, and I know more about their lives than I do about my own family, but I'm also their boss, and I always thought that put a wall between us. Maybe that had all been in my head, though. It was a shame I was only just discovering this when I was about to lose my store.

Steve's hand tentatively touches my back. "So, if Roman took advantage of you, we have your back, okay? We'll make sure he doesn't come in here again."

Panicked at where his thoughts are, I spin back to him. "No, that's not what happened." I reach up to rub my neck, and my fingers bump against the nape guard. "More like the other way around. And things are awkward now because…"

"You're friends and being lovers is too weird?" Steve guesses.

My lips part in surprise. "We're not friends."

Steve's brows sweep together in confusion. "You're not?" He glances at the empty table again. "But, he comes in every day. You even have a table reserved for him. And when you're not here, he always asks how you're doing."

Now, it's my turn to be confused. "He does?"

Steve nods slowly. "Yeah. He's been asking about you for the last week, too. Mia's been short with him, of course, but he still asks."

I scrub a hand over my face. "Sorry I put you two in the middle of this. I'll stop being a coward and talk to him."

Steve pats my shoulder in sympathy. "The longer you wait, the more awkward it gets. If you don't want to be lovers, be firm about it, and, if he's a good friend, he'll accept that and move on."

I give him an assessing look. "You sound like you're speaking from experience."

"Hey, just because I'm a Beta doesn't mean I haven't had some awkward moments in relationships. Loving someone is messy, regardless of what you are." A customer walks in, heading straight for the counter, and Steve squeezes my shoulder one last time. "I'm here to listen if you need someone to complain to about relationships."

"I appreciate that." Closing the pastry case, I return the tray to the kitchen, my thoughts swirling with uncertainty.

Can Roman and I be friends? We're adults now, and all of my reasons for not liking him are rooted in who we were as children. I'm not the same person I was back then, and after the way Roman took care of me at the auction, I'm no longer sure he's the same person, either. Even if we're not lovers, we could be *something*.

He'd asked me to meet up after work. Maybe he wants to try being friends, too?

Tomorrow, I'll buck up the courage to be on the floor when he comes in for his morning tea. If he doesn't flat out reject me on the spot, I'll see if he wants to grab dinner or something.

What's the worst that can happen, right?

I check my reflection in the small rearview mirror one more time, making sure my turtle neck covers the nape guard and adjusting the collar of the sports jacket I pulled on after I left the tea shop. It helps dress up the slacks I wore while keeping my outfit casual. I have no idea what family Mother negotiated with to marry my sister, but my attire should be fine for a casual lunch.

The clock on the dash tells me I'm fifteen minutes early, so right on time as far as Mother's concerned.

A quick comb of my fingers through my black hair sets it straight, and I climb out of my car. I parked it at the back of the house so it wouldn't be an eyesore for our guest. I'll miss the old thing when it's gone, as I'm sure it's on Mother's list of things to destroy in my life. She wants me driving that ridiculous Bentley that's been sitting neglected in the garage for the last three years.

A car worthy of a Heardst, she had said. She wanted to give me a driver to go with it, but I flat out refused the entire setup. I live in the historic district of Rockhaven, within walking distance of the tea shop and the local marketplace. I don't need a fancy car with a driver.

But that will change if I move back home.

My steps slow as I pull my cell phone from my pocket and check for any messages. I'd broken down and called my father in the hope he'd let me come stay with him and his new wife until I can find a different job and a new place to live. So far, though, he hasn't returned my call. I shouldn't get my hopes up. When he left my mom, he cut ties with the Heardst family, which included his kids.

The back door opens before I reach it, and I glance up in surprise to find the butler waiting for me. He must have seen me pull around back. He's too good for this house, and I won't be surprised if he finds a post somewhere else soon, with a family that will bother to remember his name.

"Thank you, Stirling," I say as I step inside. "Has our guest arrived?"

"Not yet, Master Heardst." He gestures toward the front of the house. "Madam and Miss Katheryn are waiting in the blue parlor."

"Thank you." I head down the hall past the formal dining room and the small ballroom to a sitting room at the front of the house.

The blue parlor earns its name from the pale blue wallpaper that covers the room. Heavy, dark-blue damask drapes frame tall windows that look out onto a side yard, and the antique couches are done in the same dark-blue fabric. The glass and gold coffee table in the center of the room holds a white china teapot with small blue flowers. Mother and Katheryn both wear dresses in pale blue that pop off the couch and accentuate their long, black hair.

Mother frowns at my green blazer and looks past me to the butler. "Archibald, please fetch my son one of the blue house jackets from the downstairs guest suite."

"I hardly think me not matching the furniture will put off Katheryn's suitor, Mother," I say.

She lifts her nose with a sniff. "We are a family; we should look like one."

No one who looks at us will question that we're related, but I hold my tongue. If changing my jacket will make her happy, it's no skin off my teeth.

I turn to Stirling. "I'll fetch the jacket. Our guest will be here soon, and we don't want him waiting on the doorstep."

"Brush your hair while you're at it," Mother calls. "You look like a ragamuffin."

Lifting a hand to let her know I heard, I head back down the hall and take a right at the ballroom, where a set of four mini-suites offer a place for drunk guests to sober up after partying too hard. The closets are kept stocked with various clothing so whoever stays over doesn't have to do a walk-of-shame home the next day in their party attire.

I find a blue jacket in my size and trade it out for my green one. The collar on it lays flatter than the one I arrived in, but the turtle neck comes up to my chin. If I look close, I can see the outline of my nape guard beneath the fabric, but no one will be looking for it. It's most obvious at the back, where the strip of leather widens to the size of my palm to support a thin metal disk that completely covers my nape. The website I ordered it from guaranteed it was bite-resistant and tamper-proof, with a lock at the back only I have the code to.

I might have gone a little overboard when I bought it, but I hadn't been thinking clearly. I'd been in the panicked *Oh-My-God-I'm-An-Omega-And-Need-To-Protect-Myself* mindset.

After a double-check that my hair's fine, I head back toward the blue parlor.

Murmurs drift out with a deeper voice mingled between my mother's and sister's high tones. Looks like our guest arrived, and I managed to be late despite my best effort.

I paste a smile on my face as I turn into the room, my eyes moving automatically to the couch opposite my family.

Cool blue eyes meet mine, and I stumble a step as Roman stands.

Panicked, I glance at my mother and sister to gauge their reaction. Did Roman grow tired of me dodging him at the tea shop and decide to come directly to the source? But how would he know I was here today? Though, I never told him I *didn't* live at the family home. He'd come here more than once in high school, as had many of our classmates, so he knew where to find me.

My mother lifts her brows inquisitively, and I turn back to Roman, desperate to defuse the situation as quickly as possible. "Roman, what are you doing here?"

His lips part, but my mother cuts in before he can answer. "Don't be rude to our guest, Warren. Hurry and pour everyone tea so we can settle down to business."

Lips numb, I turn back to her. "Business?"

She makes an impatient gesture to indicate Katheryn. "Yes, of course. Roman is here to discuss his betrothal to your sister."

8

As the floor falls out from under me, Roman's hand on my arm guides me to the couch. I sit heavily, ears ringing with my mother's words.

Roman's the man she set up to marry my *sister*? How is that even possible? Then, cold realization strikes, and I turn to give him an accusing glare. He had to have known about this before the auction, but he hadn't said anything.

God, how stupid could I be?

His hand lifts toward me, but I scoot back as far as the couch will allow, avoiding his touch. I was just thinking we could be friends. Stupid, stupid me. We'll soon be more than friends; we'll be brothers.

"Goodness, Warren, what is wrong with you?"

Mother stands to pour the tea herself, passing out the cups. "First this business at the auction, and now you're being rude to our guest. I do apologize, Roman. I don't know what has gotten into my son lately."

Roman. Roman has gotten into her son. Multiple times. In every position imaginable.

I bite back the hysterical laugh that bubbles up my throat and clutch the small teacup I hold to ground myself back in reality. A reality where Roman is going to marry my *sister*.

Roman takes his cup but immediately stands to set it back on the coffee table. When he settles on the couch once more, he takes the middle cushion, his leg pressing against mine. "Yes, we were just discussing this betrothal business. As I said, there seems to have been a misunderstanding."

"Is it the addendum?" Mother sits next to Katheryn and puts a hand on her knee. "Surely you can understand the toll childbearing puts on a person, both mentally and physically. An additional monthly allowance is a trifle compared to the joy of parenthood."

Katheryn nods as she leans back on the sofa. She delicately lifts a hand to her stomach as if already able to imagine the multitude of children she'll have with Roman.

A sour knot forms in my stomach, and I clutch my teacup tighter, willing myself not to puke. This can't be happening. I don't want to be here while they barter over the price of babies.

"I'd hardly call ten-thousand a month per child a trifle." Roman holds up a hand to stop her protest. "But I'm not going to argue over that."

A satisfied smile spreads over my mother's face. "I'm so glad you see our side of things."

Roman frowns and glances at me. "I'm afraid I have a much *larger* issue with this proposal."

"Surely it's not so large an issue that we can't work through it. You did come today, after all, which means you're willing to negotiate." She lifts her cup, taking a tiny sip, before her nose wrinkles, and she sets it down. "Goodness, Warren, if this is a representation of the tea you sell, it's no wonder your business was failing."

Frowning, I take a drink of tea and promptly spit it back in the cup. Coconut oil coats my tongue, along with sticky sweet sugar and an overwhelming taste of peppermint. Quickly, I lean forward to set the cup on the coffee table. "That's not tea. That's the sugar scrub I gave Katheryn."

"Really, you should label these things better."

Mother takes the cup Katheryn holds and calls out, "Archibald, please bring lemonade for our guest."

"I didn't know you were planning to expand." Roman gives me a warm smile. "Is it just sugar scrubs, or do you have a whole line planned?"

"It was going to be a natural spa line." I shake my head. "But it doesn't matter. It's not going to happen."

He leans closer, his smoky voice lowered just for me. "Don't be so ready to give up."

Of course, that's when my memory decides to draw up all the other times that smokey voice filled my ear recently as Roman pushed into my body, his honeyed words filling me with stupid ideas.

As if his mind went to the same place, Roman leans back, his arms spreading over the back of the couch. Out of view of the others, his fingers brush the collar of my turtle neck, raising goose bumps all over my body. Now is not the time to pop a boner, though, and I subtly dig my elbow into his side to make him stop.

He ignores me to focus on my mother. "Back to business. When your proposal first came in, I agreed to consider it because I was under the impression my preferences were clear."

My mother's lips purse. "I can assure you, Katheryn is fully capable of bearing Alpha children."

Roman lifts his free hand to brush that aside while his other hand slips beneath the collar of my turtle neck. I try to shift away, but he persists, and when he encounters the nape guard, his finger slips beneath that, too, tracing the Mark still on my neck. "I'm talking about my sexual preferences, Ms. Heardst. I've never hidden the fact that I'm gay, and that anyone I married would, of course, need to be a man."

My mother's eyes narrow as they shift between us, but Roman continues before she can speak. "I was pleasantly surprised that the Heardst family was seeking a union with my family, so I was rather shocked when I ran into Warren at the Wellington Charity Auction, stepping out with someone else."

My pulse jumps, the nausea I felt earlier being pushed aside by something else.

Katheryn leans forward, all hint of her delicate facade vanishing. "Are you saying you thought you were accepting a proposal from *Warren*?"

Roman's finger continues to stroke over his Mark. "Indeed, I did."

"But he's an Alpha." Katheryn points at me accusingly. "He can't give you heirs the way I can."

"That is a topic between Warren and me." Roman's thumb strokes over my racing pulse. "I'd like to discuss with him—"

"No," my mother's sharp voice cuts him off. "Warren is not available. I am already in discussion with another family who is eager to move forward—"

The pleasantness melts from Roman's expression. "Cancel it."

"You don't have a say in this matter." Mother thrusts to her feet. "If you are not interested in Katheryn, then we have nothing left to discuss."

Roman doesn't budge from his place beside me. "That's not your decision to make, and Warren has already given me his response."

Shocked, I turn to stare at him. When did he ask me to marry him?

Then, his hand moves on my neck, and I realize he's not talking about marriage. He's talking about Marking me, and anger simmers through my blood. He spent our entire time in high school proving he's better than me, and now he's going to swoop in and take control of my life just because I bear his Mark?

Shoving his hand away, I stand and stare down at him. "I never agreed to marry you, and I sure as hell won't be bought with some agreement you make with my mother."

"Warren…"

When he reaches for my hand, I jerk it away. "I

can't believe you! Is there something wrong with your head? Is this you finally *winning*?"

He stands slowly. "You're rejecting me?"

"What's there to reject?" I throw my hands up. "You haven't even *asked* me!"

Angry now himself, he steps closer with a low growl. "I did! You said yes!"

His scent grows heavier, curling around me, and I shove against his chest to put space between us, but the man's solid as a brick and doesn't budge. "You never asked!"

Reaching up, he hooks a finger in my turtle neck, yanking it down to expose my nape guard. "Then why are you protecting my Mark?"

Breathing heavily, I step back from him. "It's a *guard*, you idiot. So it won't happen again!"

Silence falls over the room as we breathe heavily. Roman looks ready to throw me down and test how tamper-proof my nape guard is, and part of me wants to push him to do it. His angry eyes drop to my mouth, and heat flushes my neck, crawling toward my cheeks. Over those three days together, my body learned to respond to this man, to reach for him to fulfill my needs.

Determination darkens his eyes, and he takes a step forward to close the distance between us.

"*Stop*," my mother Commands.

The weight of the word rolls right over Roman. She's not as strong an Alpha as he is; I know it in the way he finishes the movement, leaving only a hand's breadth between us before he turns to face her. "My apologies for yelling, Ms. Heardst."

He turns back to me, and for a moment, I think he'll reach for me to finish what he started.

But his hands clench at his sides. "I'll leave for today. This is a conversation meant to be private. I'll contact you later, Warren." Then, as if he can't help himself, he turns back to my mother. "My claim on Warren is in effect for three more weeks. I trust you won't breach the Alpha Code in this."

Her mouth drops open in shock as Roman spins on his heel and strides from the room.

Left alone with the wolves, all attention turns on me, and my mother snaps her mouth closed with a click before she demands, "Why is my Alpha son wearing a nape guard? And what did Roman mean when he said he Marked you?"

9

Resigned, I turn to face my family. I knew I couldn't hide it forever, but I also hadn't planned for my new status to come out like this. "So, it turns out I'm an Omega."

"Impossible." Mother slashes her hand through the air as if that will wipe away my words. "We haven't had anything but Alphas for five generations."

"It's true. I've been to a doctor to verify."

"Some small-time hack, obviously." She pulls her cell phone from her pocket. "I'll have Dr. Holt come out. He can bring a sedative as well. I'm going to need it after the headache you've caused."

Before I can protest, she paces out of the room, the phone already pressed to her ear. I could have shown her my Mark, or the pack of suppressants I carry around because I'm not yet confident enough to know when my next Heat will come on. But I don't bother. She won't believe I'm an Omega until her own people confirm it.

Sighing, I settle back onto the sofa, and Roman's scent surrounds me, prickling at my senses. He wasn't here for long, but traces of bergamot and spice linger in the air. It makes me want to run after him, to drag him off to bed where we can just let our bodies do the talking.

From the way he acted, he still wants me, something I hadn't expected without my Heat being involved. Hell, he even wants to marry me? I scrub my hands over my face. How did this happen? The whole world's been turned upside down.

When I straighten, I find Katheryn staring at me from across the coffee table, her hazel eyes shrewd. "If Roman Marked you, that means you've already bedded him. How did you wrangle that encounter? That must have taken some planning on your part, to put yourself in his path right when your Heat came on. How long has that been going on, anyway? Were you already fucking him before Mother set up the contract with Mr. Freely, or did you seek Roman out in the hope of escaping that marriage?"

Anger burns through me. "I didn't set out to

seduce Roman. And I didn't have to put myself in his path. I know where he is every single day."

Her eyes widen in shock. "You've been *stalking* him as well? Are you really so desperate?"

"What? No!" I lower my voice as Stirling walks in, carrying a tray with four tall glasses of lemonade.

We stay silent as he cleans up the tea service and disappears as quietly as he came.

My upbringing kicks in, and I rise to pass Katheryn a glass before taking one for myself and settling back on the couch. I take a sip, letting the tart drink cool my anger before I face my sister once more. "No, I'm not stalking him. Roman comes into the tea shop on his way to work every day."

Her brows pinch together. "But doesn't he work at Markham Marketing?"

"As far as I know." I take another sip of lemonade. "He hasn't mentioned changing jobs."

"They built a new office in uptown two years ago. Your tea shop is nowhere near Roman's workplace." She shakes her head. "He must be a tea snob to keep going out of his way."

Unsettled, I focus on the condensation on the outside of my glass. Roman really isn't a tea snob. He puts so much honey in his earl grey that he can't even taste the quality of the leaves. He could have the same experience by buying the pre-bagged stuff available at the supermarket for a fraction of the price. Why would he go out of his way to continue to frequent my store?

I have a feeling it has something to do with things he said while I was lost to the fever of my first Heat. Was it possible he didn't just ask to Mark me back then, but had asked for something even deeper? But why? He's never been kind to me.

Except that he has. Not just during my Heat, either.

If I let my thoughts settle on Roman—something I strive not to allow—I realize Roman hasn't been the show-off from high school that I remember him being. I had chalked that up to no longer being in class or sports together. But as I rack my memory for our interactions over the last five years, the only time he's chafed my nerves is when he criticized my store, and it's possible I was just over-sensitive about sound advice offered by someone raised to live and breathe marketing. Yeah, he could have been less blunt in his delivery, but the tips helped improve my business.

Mother strides back into the room, saving me the headache of trying to untangle my emotions where Roman's concerned.

Her cold gaze lands on me. "Dr. Holt will be here soon. You should prepare for the exam in your room."

"Sure, no problem." I stand and head for the door. "But after that, I need to leave. I have work in the morning."

"You'll meet with me first," she says sharply. "We have much to discuss about your future if this turns out to be true. It changes our options."

I can practically see the finance sheets unrolling through her mind, running analysis on the net profit of families like Herold's, who have the wealth to become part of the upper-class but lack the pedigree background to make that final step without marriage.

Jaw clenched against the words I want to say to her, I leave the room and head upstairs.

My room on the second floor hasn't changed since I left for university and never came back. It still holds the posters of sports teams I'd been into, and books on herbs, spices, and flavor profiles tucked under my bed like a dirty secret. Growing up, I'd been expected to be a socialite like my mother and sister, providing to the community through philanthropy over actual work.

Why work when we were ridiculously wealthy?

Now, my 'silly hobby' makes me the only one in this family not only willing, but actually capable, of living without our wealth. Too bad my plans hadn't quite taken off. Roman was right when he said I got my start from my parents, that I still relied on them. No bank would have given me a loan to open a tea shop right out of university without any prior experience.

I'd taken the easier route and accepted the money from my family, and now that was biting me in the ass. Both figuratively and literally, if Mother has her way and sells me off.

I walk over to the small display case that houses the few trophies I won in school. Most are second-place or runner-up, but there were a few times mine and Roman's interests diverged, where I managed some first-place prizes. Like in cooking class. I touch the blue ribbon. I'd won that one for my jumbo snicker-doodle cookies, the same recipe I sell in the shop.

A light tap comes from the open door, and I turn to find Dr. Holt standing in the opening, a medical bag in one hand. Mother hovers behind him, but I close the door in her face before she can sit in on the exam. There's only so far she can push, and seeing me naked is a hard no for me.

"Good afternoon, Warren." Dr. Holt sets his bag on the desk against one wall. "So, your mother tells me you think you're an Omega?"

"I *know* I am. I've already been to see a doctor to have it confirmed." Showing him the suppressants, I punch in the code for my nape guard by feel and unlatch it.

Dr. Hold sets my prescription aside and his cool, dry fingers move my turtle neck aside. "This is how old?"

"A week." I focus on the floor. "It's the first."

"It's healing well, and the impression is clear. Your Alpha shows a good level of self-restraint." He steps back. "It was consensual?"

"As much as anything during a Heat is consensual." I gesture to his bag. "Do you really need to perform an exam?"

He pulls out a stethoscope. "I'd like to check your heart and lungs, take your temperature… Did you use condoms?"

My cheeks heat as I shake my head. I'm not a prude, but I've been seeing Dr. Holt since I was in diapers. "I already had a pregnancy test. It came back negative."

The gentle smile he gives me forms deep wrinkles around his eyes. "We should take another blood test in a week, just to be sure. Sometimes you can get a false negative when it's this early." He fits the stethoscope around his neck. "But as for a full exam, no, we don't need one. The Mark on your neck is proof enough. If it were an Alpha biting another Alpha, or even a Beta, the Mark wouldn't be healing so fast. It's already sinking beneath your skin."

My hand lifts to touch my nape. I'd been surprised how quickly the scab washed off, and my skin feels smooth to the touch, now. I haven't been brave enough to look at it in the mirror, though. Looking makes it real, and I've been trying hard to pretend what happened between Roman and me was a fever dream. Otherwise, I find myself rolling over in the middle of the night, reaching for someone who isn't there.

"Did your other doctor talk to you about the precautions you'll need to take now?" Dr. Holt asks as he checks my heartbeat. When I nod, he moves to press the stethoscope to my back. "Deep breaths."

Dr. Holt completes his exam and takes a vial of blood for testing, and we make an appointment for me to drop into his office next week for another pregnancy test.

When I walk him out of my bedroom, I find my mother still waiting in the hall, as if she feared I'd escape before she had a chance to sink her hooks back into me.

Dr. Holt hands her a summary report as he passes,

along with a bottle of what I assume are tranquilizers. Come eight o'clock tonight, she'll be passed out and won't wake up for anything until morning.

When I try to follow the doctor to the stairs, Mother latches onto my arm, steering me to her private study instead.

She closes the door and strides to her credenza, where she picks up a stack of printouts. So, she hadn't been hovering outside my door the whole time. No, she'd been busily printing out future marriage candidates.

"I don't know how this happened, but it seems fate is looking out for our family. Your status as an Omega significantly broadens our options for your future spouse." The corners of her lips tighten. "But don't get your hopes up about Roman. His family name is too good to expect them to refill our bank accounts by marrying him. We can find someone better, in need of the Heardst name and desperate for a male Omega."

The calculating way she discusses my future, as if I have no say in it, makes my stomach roll.

She flips through the papers she holds. "Now, the Filbert family—the east coast, not the west coast—has a son who's about to take over the family business. He's in need of a spouse to help soothe the shareholder's opinion that he's a bit of a wild child. A child of his own will help with that."

The sinking sensation in my stomach grows. "Mother—"

"Or there's the Wellington's," she continues without pause. "Their hotel chain has done quite well, and they're looking to make connections to expand—"

"Mother!" I yell to stop her.

She frowns at me. "Really, Warren, there's no need to raise your voice. I'm right here."

My heart pounds with panic, but I can't pretend I'm okay with this anymore. "I'm not going to marry one of those men."

"You haven't even looked at them, yet."

"It doesn't matter." I back toward the door. "I'm not going to sell myself to the highest bidder."

Her eyes narrow on me. "You'll abandon your family, the same way your father did?"

The words land like arrows in my chest, and I stop next to the door, my hand on the knob. "I'm not cutting ties with you, but I'm also not willing to marry for business. I know that worked for you and that Katheryn is happy with a similar arrangement, but I want *more* from my future spouse."

"What, like *love*?" she scoffs.

"Yes, exactly like that." For the first time in my life, I pity my mother, because she's never felt a deep, emotional bond for anyone in her life. Otherwise, she wouldn't be so quick to sell her children's futures to the highest bidder. "I want to look forward to seeing my husband in the morning and when I come home at night. I want someone I can call when I'm happy or sad, to know that they'll be there for me."

"Then take a lover on the side, just like everyone else does. Don't marry for *love*." Her lip curls in disgust. "Love is just passion, and passion fades. A marriage made with business in mind will last because emotions aren't involved."

But it hadn't lasted for her. I don't point that out, though. Nothing I say will change her mind.

"I'm sorry." I open the door. "This isn't me abandoning you and Katheryn; I'll always be a call away if you need me. But I won't be marrying anyone to help the family out."

"*Warren, come back here*," she Commands, but the words sweep right over me.

She doesn't have the power to stop me anymore. Not while my Alpha protects me. And that's what Roman is right now. *My Alpha*. For better or worse, I belong to him for as long as his Mark lasts. And I now realize I may not be as opposed to it lasting as I told myself I was.

Softly, I shut the door behind me and walk out of the family home. Whether or not I'll be welcome back is up in the air, but it won't be me who stops calling.

Before me, my future stretches murky with uncertainty, but I know one thing for sure. Whatever happens next will be of my choosing, and nothing else matters.

10

On Sunday, I go into work and tell Steve and Mia what's happening. I should have done that as soon as I received the notice that the shop had been sold, but I was too much in my own head to look at those around me.

They take the news of the eventual closure better than expected, both surprising me when they offer to stay on until after the changeover, even though it leaves their futures as uncertain as mine.

On the drive back to my apartment yesterday, I had realized how I let my family drive me into a corner through fear. Marrying me off for money isn't the family's only option. Hell, Mother can marry some rich old Alpha if she wants to keep her position in society.

I just wish I realized that from the beginning.

With my degree in business and five years of experience running my a store, it won't be hard to find a new job. I'll likely even make more money without the expense of building up my business. It will suck, but I'm not as locked in as Mother convinced me I was.

For the first time since she dropped the bomb on us, my thoughts are finally clear. I'm no longer in desperate-scramble mode. Steve offered me the use of his spare bedroom while I job hunt, and I swallow my pride, promising to pay him back once I figure things out.

I spend the rest of the night packing up my meager belongings. I have another week before I have to be out, and I want to be ready.

When Monday comes, I feel calm. The new owner will arrive to look over the place and hopefully inform us of when he'll be closing the doors. If it's an option, I'd like to stay open through the end of the month to have time to sell the products we have on hand and give everyone time to find new jobs. But if the doors close tonight and don't open again, we're all okay with that, too.

Not even Roman strolling in for his morning tea can kill my calm.

I take the cup of sweetened earl grey and his two biscotti over to his table and drop them off with a smile on my face.

He eyes me warily. "You look like you're in a good mood, while I haven't slept a wink since Saturday."

Unapologetic for my part in that, I offer him a shrug. "Big things are happening today."

He glances around the store. "Good things?"

I shrug again. "Don't know yet."

Reaching out, he catches my hand. "Warren, we need to talk."

Some of my calm fizzles, but I push through it. "Not now. Come back after we close."

He hesitates for a moment before he nods. "Okay. Would you like to get dinner or something?"

I shake my head. "No, you can come back to my place. We can order Chinese delivery. You still like moo shu pork, right?"

A smile tugs at his lips. "You remember?"

"How can I forget? You were an asshole and always ate all the pancakes." My jab lacks its usual sting, and Roman's smile widens.

"At least you're forewarned." Reluctantly, he lets me go. "I won't take any more of your time. I'll come by at seven tonight?"

Nodding, I walk back to the counter.

Roman leaves at nine on the dot, and over the rest of the day, the calm bubble that surrounds me slowly dissolves. The new owner never comes in, and I double-check the letter to make sure I didn't mix up the date.

As I walk Mia out after closing, uncertainty fills me. I thought I'd close up tonight with a firmer idea of what my future would hold, and not knowing leaves me unsteady. Not a feeling I enjoy as I search the line of parked cars for Roman. I don't even know what he drives. Probably something fast and flashy.

"Warren!" a voice calls, and I turn to see Roman jogging down the street toward me. "Sorry, I'm late. The bus was running behind schedule."

My brows lift. "You use the bus?"

Grinning, he stops next to me. "It gives me time to read."

"Huh." I turn toward my apartment, and he falls into step beside me.

"Did you want me to drive? I'll call a taxi." He pulls out his phone, but I push it back toward his pocket.

"I live nearby. We can pick up the food on the way, if you don't mind?" The Chinese restaurant takes forty minutes to deliver or ten minutes to pick up.

"Sounds good." He tucks his hands into his

pockets, and the air between us turns awkward before he ventures, "Did you have a good day at work?"

"We were busy," I say shortly, then wince. The response didn't exactly invite further questions, but we've never done this before, and I've never been good with small talk.

He doesn't respond, and we walk in silence for a block before my good manners kick in. "Did *you* have a good day at work?"

"It was busy." He looks out at the passing cars and lets out a sigh. "This is harder than I thought it would be. What did we use to talk about all the time?"

I frown. "We didn't."

He turns back to me with a frown of his own. "Yes, we did. We were always talking."

"We were always antagonizing each other," I clarify.

Roman searches my face and sighs again. "Well, *I* was talking."

"Are you trying to pick a fight?" I demand.

His brows lift. "Are *you*?"

I kind of am. It's the only way I know how to talk to Roman, and I find myself *wanting* to talk. I just don't know what to say.

At the next block, we turn left, and Roman's hand

knocks against mine. Startled, I look at him, but he stares at the sidewalk, lost in thought.

At the Chinese restaurant, we place our order and sip on cups of green tea as we wait.

Roman adds sugar to his and grimaces. "Your tea is better."

That pulls a laugh from me. "It's a completely different type of tea."

"Are you saying not all weeds are the same?" he teases. When I mock-scowl at him, he leans forward. "So, tell me all the ways that earl grey and green tea are different, oh god of tea."

"Just remember you asked for this," I warn before launching into the growing, harvesting, and drying process of tea leaves.

The topic carries us through the server dropping off our to-go order and all the way back to my apartment. Roman carries the bag of food, leaving me free to gesture as I talk. I expected him to zone out within five minutes, but he's actually interested, asking pointed questions that keep the topic rolling.

He's better at this socializing thing than I am.

As he steps inside, and we kick off our shoes, he glances around the small, box-filled space. "Are you going somewhere?"

"I'm being evicted at the end of the month." I move a box aside to make room for our food.

He frowns as he shrugs out of his jacket. "Did you miss your rent payment?"

I shake my head. "I leased the place under my family name. Mother canceled the contract."

Not looking at me, he pulls the food containers from the bag. "She's really determined to force you to fall in line, isn't she?"

Pulling two plates from the cabinet I haven't packed yet, I set them on the table. "She's going to be disappointed."

"You're not moving back home, then?" Though he sounds casual, tension runs through his shoulders.

"No," I say slowly.

His head stays down. "And her hunt for your perfect spouse?"

"Don't worry, you're off the hook for that." I study the top of his head. "I won't be auctioning myself off."

He forces a laugh. "That's good, because I really didn't want to pay ten-thousand a month for a kid. There are far better ways to spend that kind of money."

"Oh?" I pop open the container of thin pancakes and take half before he can steal them all. "What will you do with all that spare cash now?"

Without looking up, he takes the remaining pancakes. "Investment it in something meaningful."

Curiosity gets the better of me. "What's more meaningful than kids?"

"Dreams." His eyes lift to meet mine. "A tea shop."

The blood drains from my face, and I grip the table for support. "*You're* the new owner?"

"Investor," he corrects. "I don't know anything about tea. That's all on you."

Slowly, I sink into one of the chairs. "Why did you do that?"

Roman scrubs a hand through his hair, mussing the auburn locks. "I'm apparently *really* bad at this, so I'm just going to say it." Striding forward, he kneels in front of me and takes my limp hands. "Warren Heardst, I'm in love with you."

"Bullshit," I whisper, too shocked for my brain to come up with anything else.

Roman's eyes narrow. "Not *only* am I in love with you, but I think you feel the same."

"Double bullshit." I tug my hands free. "You don't love me. You think of me as your rival."

Undeterred, he grasps my knees. "Every single guy you've dated has looked just like me. That can't be a coincidence."

"I don't..." My brain flashes all my blue-eyed, auburn-haired boyfriends in front of my eyes. "I just have a type." Then I glare at the man in front of me. "And you *stole* all of them away."

His thumbs rub circles on my thighs. "Did it make you sad?"

"It pissed me off!"

His fingers slip under my knees. "But did it make you *sad*?"

I lick my lips, not wanting to admit it didn't. What kind of horrible person does that make me that I wasn't sad when my boyfriends ditched me for someone else? I was just angry that Roman won yet again.

"It didn't, did it?" He tugs on my legs, pulling me lower in the seat before he pushes them open to make room for himself. "It didn't make you sad because none of them was the man you really wanted to be with."

Shaking my head, my eyes drop to his lips. "You were always competing against me."

"I was doing my best to prove I was good enough to be with you." His hands stroke up my thighs to my hips. "I didn't realize it was driving you away until it was too late."

My heart races, but I ignore it. "So, you thought you'd *buy* me instead?"

"I've been courting you for *five years*, Warren." He gives a self-deprecating smile. "I'll admit, I've been doing it *badly*, but I've been *trying*. Was it so foolish of me to think that a marriage contract was a sign?"

"But I'm an Alpha," I protest.

"No, you're not. You're an Omega. *My* Omega." He rises on his knees, his bergamot and citrus scent surrounding me. "But even if you were an Alpha, I wouldn't care." Gaze holding mine, he leans forward until his lips brush mine. "Alpha, Omega, Beta, I don't care. I just want *you*. I always have." I shiver as each word teases an almost-kiss. "Tell me I'm alone in this. Tell me there's no chance for me, and I'll walk away. I'll never bother you again. You can keep running the tea shop; I'll stay as a silent partner, and you can buy it back whenever you want, no strings attached."

My gut clenches with panic. I don't want him to stop coming to the tea shop. I don't want to stop seeing him every day.

He brushes his lips across mine again. "You're not pushing me away. Does that mean I can take that as a sign?"

I try to speak, but the words won't come.

Slowly, Roman pulls back. "Or should I go?"

Groaning in protest, I close the distance between us, my mouth covering his.

11

My mouth opens at the first brush of Roman's tongue, and he sweeps in, laying claim to me all over again.

How could I have walked away from this a week ago? How could I not recognize his feelings in the tender way he cups my cheek, in the way he tugs me closer?

Gasping, I pull back. "Ask me."

"What?" His hands slip under my shirt.

"I'm not confused by the Heat now." Lifting my arms, I let him pull my shirt over my head. "Ask me what you did before."

His fingers slip beneath the nape guard to brush against my Mark. "Let me take care of you. Let me love you. Let me Mark you and marry you, and be with you always."

"Yes." I pepper kisses across his face. "Long engagement, lots of dates to get to know each other, and if we survive that, then yes."

"Anything you need." He pulls my lips back to his. "Just remember, I'm really bad at this whole love thing."

"We'll get better together." I thread my fingers through his hair to pull him closer. "Tomorrow. We'll get better tomorrow. My bedroom's down the hall."

Roman doesn't waste any time lifting me from the chair and into his arms, striding to my bedroom.

We tumble onto the bed, Roman's body covering mine, and I moan as he manhandles me into the position he wants with my legs spread and him firmly between them. His hard cock grinds against mine as his hands slide over my chest and waist.

Hot lips find my ear. "I missed you so much."

At the sharp nip of his teeth, a gasp escapes me. "It was only a week."

"I've wanted you for thirteen years. A week longer is too much." He licks a hot line down my throat to catch my nape guard between his teeth, tugging gently. "I want this off."

Groaning, I loop one leg around his waist. "Not until we're married."

He gives it another sharp tug before he releases it. "I'll call a judge tonight."

I tug his hair, trying to pull his mouth back to mine. "And get out of bed?"

"Tomorrow." Ignoring my urging, he shifts lower. "I'll call a judge tomorrow."

"You promised me a long enga—" A moan cuts me off as his mouth finds my hard shaft through my pants.

Roman glances up my body with a wicked smile. "Long engagement, or you in my mouth?"

In answer, I reach down and unzip my pants.

He growls with approval before his head bows, his beautiful lips folding over me. The heat of his mouth surrounds my aching tip, and he tongues my slit, licking away my pre-cum before he takes me deeper, all the way into his throat. I moan at the tight flex of muscles around my hard dick, my fingers driving into his hair to tug fitfully. It feels good, but I need more. I need movement and suction. I need his lips red with friction and slick with drool and cum.

I pull his hair harder until his head lifts, then thrust up into his mouth, loving the stretch of his lips around me and the way he willingly takes me back in.

His hands move to my hips, urging me to fuck his mouth. Gasping, I watch myself moving in and out from between his lips, pleasure filling me every time I slide into his throat, every time his tongue presses against the large vein on the underside of my dick.

A tingle starts in my toes and works its way up my legs, tightening my muscles with pleasure. Sensing how close I am, Roman takes back control, his cheeks hollowing with suction as his head bobs faster. My hands fist in his thick hair as my thighs tense, my balls tingling before a pulse of pleasure rolls through me. Cum shoots from my dick, and Roman's throat works around me, swallowing it down.

Sucking hard as he pulls back, he licks the last drop of cum from my tip before he releases me.

Pulse still racing, I lay limp and gasping on the bed as I try to catch my breath.

Roman sits back on his heels, his fingers hooking in my waistband before he strips off my pants. He pushes my legs apart and bends once more, his mouth on my sensitive balls as one hand slips farther back to find my entrance.

When he finds me already wet, he groans, his fingers pushing inside me. Unlike during my Heat, my body resists the invasion, the stretch of tight muscles burning, and he's gentle and patient as he loosens me until I can take four of his fingers.

By then, I'm shifting restlessly, my dick thickening once more with desire. This is different from when I was overcome with fever. Back then, I'd been driven to mate, willing to skip all the fun stuff to have Roman in me as fast as possible, and he'd been the same, pushed by instinct to ease my need.

But now, he doesn't rush, even when he has me stretched open for him. Instead, he kisses his way back up my body, stopping to linger at my nipples and tug playfully on my nape guard before sucking the skin above it into his mouth.

Moaning, I tug at his clothes, not liking that he still has them on while I'm fully naked. The fabric scratches at my sensitive skin, chaffing against my dick and nipples.

I tug at the back of his shirt. "Off."

"Undress me," he counters, his voice a smoky purr in my ear.

He sits back once more, taking his delicious weight off me, and I follow him up, my fingers fumbling with the buttons of his shirt. I want to rip the damn thing open to reach the hot body beneath, but I force myself to undo them one-by-one until I can push it off his shoulders and throw it to the floor.

He sits back farther as I get to work on his belt then the button and fly on his slacks, lifting his hips when I pull them down.

It's like unwrapping the best present ever, the only one no one but Roman can give me. His muscular body, bared and sprawled out on my comforter, makes my breath catch. I can't believe this man is mine, that I'll get to argue with and love him for the rest of my life.

"Come here," he growls, pulling me to straddle his hips.

My hands land on his hard stomach, my legs spread wide in the unfamiliar position. The world feels different on top of Roman, like there was a shift in power. Eyes wide, I look down at him, not sure what he expects.

Heated gaze locked on me, his hands smooth up my thighs. "Put me inside of you."

My thighs flex at his words, and his hard cock nudges against my ass. Heart pounding, I lift onto my knees and reach back to fist his cock, holding it steady as I sink onto him. The first stretch of muscles burns as his width spreads me open, and I gasp at the sheer size of him. In my Heat, I had no problem taking him all at once, but now, I have to work to fit him in, my hips rocking in short thrusts as my body struggles to accommodate him.

The sensation feels different from my Heat, too. I feel more of him now, the soft head of his cock forging a pathway for the steely strength of his shaft. He feels hot and pulsing inside me, and my muscles flex and squeeze around his hard length, relearning his shape.

My hips move faster, the drag of him in and out of my body almost too intense. Biting my lip, I lean back, one hand moving to his thigh, and his cock drags against the tight bundle of nerves inside of me. My dick jerks at the added pleasure, cum seeping from my tip, and Roman smears his hand through it before gripping my dick.

I moan, hips moving faster, overwhelmed by the sensation of my dick dragging from his hand as his cock fills my body, then thrusting back into the tight cup of his fist as his cock slides out.

Roman bends his knees, thrusting up on my next downward swing, and I cry out at the deeper penetration. I know he rode me harder during my Heat, but it had never felt this deep, this invasive, like his cock was reaching up into my stomach. I lift a hand, pressing it over my lower abdomen to see if I can feel him there, but Roman pulls my hand away, wrapping my fingers around my dick before his hands grip my hips, directing me to a harder pace as he thrusts up into me.

Frantic, I pump my shaft, thumb sweeping over my sensitive head, gathering the cum there for added lube. The tingles start again, and my head falls back, my mouth open on a moan as I roll my hips, swirling Roman's cock deep inside of me. His gasps join mine, his hands urgent on my body, pushing me down as he shoves upward.

The orgasm sweeps through me, my cum hot as it spills over my hand, and Roman pulses deep inside of me. My hips jerk, my ass rippling around him, milking out all of his cum.

Slowly, I sag forward, my face burying in the curve of his neck, and I catch my breath, filling my lungs with his unique scent and the musky smell of our passion.

He strokes a hand down my back, soothing away the aftershocks that ripple through me.

Warm lips press against my sweaty temple. "I love you." His next kiss falls on my cheek. "I love you so much."

I push myself up on trembling arms to stare down at him. "You better make me happy."

"I will," he promises. "The happiest man in

existence."

I lean down to nip at his lips. "That's a tall order. Sure you can pull it off?"

He cups my cheek, his expression tender. "Haven't I always won when I put my mind to it?"

"You do have a record to uphold." I give him a lazy, wet kiss. "But then, I wouldn't expect anything less from the man I love."

Groaning, he grips my waist and rolls until I lay beneath him. "I want to make a baby now."

I clench my ass around his softening cock. "You'll have to put more effort into it. I'm not fertile again for another three weeks."

He pushes up onto his elbows to stare down at me. "Do you really want to? Have babies with me?"

"Well, at ten-thousand a month—"

Growling, he swoops down to claim my lips in a heated kiss that sets my pulse racing once more.

When he pulls back, I reach up to cup his face. "Yes, I want a family with you. *After* all the dating and the wedding."

He frowns down at me. "You agreed to marry me tomorrow. We can go on dates afterward."

My brows lift. "No, I just unzipped my pants. It's not my fault you assumed."

His eyes narrow at the challenge. "It's going to be like this for the rest of our lives, isn't it?"

"It is," I agree.

"I can't wait." And he swoops back down to claim my lips once more.

12

Eight months later, Roman finally drags me in front of a judge.

We hold a small ceremony at the tea shop, much to my mother's horror. We closed the store early for the event and only invited close friends.

She brings along her new husband, and they stand on opposite sides of the room from each other. I doubt she'll hold onto this one for long, but at least she's stopped harping on me and Roman for choosing to live in a small, two-bedroom apartment halfway between our two jobs instead of in one of the family houses.

Katheryn had decided to skip my wedding in favor of a cruise around the world, which my mother's new husband paid for. It makes me sad, but I hadn't expected her to come. She was still on the hunt for a spouse with money and was bitter I'd 'taken' Roman from her.

Not that she ever had a chance with him.

Roman's parents came as well, and from the way they hold hands and their eyes linger on each other, I know where Roman inherited his romantic side and the perseverance to not give up on me for all those years.

My heart swells with love and happiness as I stand next to him before the judge. I'd taken his Mark for the third time a few months ago, and I now wear it with pride for all the world to see. Beyond that, my shift from Alpha to Omega hasn't affected much in my life aside from one major change.

As if he senses my thoughts, Roman's arm wraps around my waist, his palm spreading over the small swell in my stomach. The news came the month after I agreed to set a wedding date. We haven't told my mother yet. We'll leave *that* scandal for when I go in for my c-section three months ahead of schedule.

Maybe it will help her get over the fact that I refused to accept any sort of groom's gift from Roman's family. I don't want money to be between us when we start our new life, and Roman had understood that, even if my family didn't.

The judge fixes Roman with a stern look. "Do you, Roman Markham, take Warren Heardst as your lawfully wedded husband? Through sickness and health, until death do you part?"

Roman straightens, his shoulders pulling back. "I do."

The judge turns to me. "And do you, Warren Heardst, take Roman Markham as your lawfully wedded husband? Through sickness and health, until death do you part?"

I turn to Roman, my heart swelling with love. "I do."

Roman doesn't wait for the judge's go-ahead before he pulls me into his arms, his mouth finding mine with practiced ease.

As he should. He's been kissing me every day for eight months straight.

I grab his lapels and tug him closer, my lips dueling with his to see who comes out the winner.

This is my high school nemesis and the owner of my heart, after all, and I plan for the first kiss of our marriage to set the standard for the rest of our life together.

The End.

Continue the series with Herold's story, Maybe Tomorrow, book 2 in Marked by His Alpha series, which features white knight alpha, hurt comfort, and age gap.

MAYBE TOMORROW

MARKED BY HIS ALPHA BOOK 2

Rich, breedable, and destined for a marriage of convenience. As an Omega, that's all Herold is to his father, but dare he dream for more?

Herold Freely has a problem. His dad keeps trying to marry him off to anyone with an old family name who needs their pockets filled the Freely fortune in exchange for a step up in society.

So far, he's managed to scare every suitor away, but his dad's tired of his inability to land a husband and takes matters into his own hands.

In steps Peter, his knight in shining armor, if only the man will stop treating Herold like he's breakable. Herold has dated enough men to know when he wants one's attention, and Peter definitely has his.

But is there even a chance of them being together? Or will he be pulled back into his father's plans for a political marriage?

READ NOW

ABOUT THE AUTHOR

Sophie O'Dare is the alter ego of paranormal and sci-fi author Lyn Forester.

She loves writing stories about guys falling in love with each other and all the shenanigans that go along with romance!

www.SophieODare.com

REVIEWS

"This is an amazing coming of age story. There are authors that you know you can depend on to fill certain reading desires you may have. You know who to go to if you want a strong heroine or an action-packed story, sexy times or teenage angst. When you pick up a book by Lyn Forester you know that you are going to be transported into another world."

— Amazon Reviewer for *You to Me*

"I loved Warren so much-- he's determined, smart, and able to weather all of his family's manipulations and to face some pretty life-changing truths about himself with aplomb. I love that he never stops advocating for himself and does everything, even falling in love with the last person he expects to, on his own terms. Well worth checking out, and hopefully, there will be more books in this universe!"

— Amazon Reviewer for *Bad With Love*

"Once I started reading this I couldn't put it down! "

— Amazon Reviewer for *As You Are*

"WARNING: DON'T START BEFORE BED!!! I stayed up way to late to finish this book. I love how Lyn's characters are multi-dimensional and the world building is unique and complex. She doesn't disappoint with this next installment in the Tails x Horns series. If you love romance, give this book a try...even if you have never done MM romance before. It was absolutely stunning."

— Amazon Reviewer for *Just Not You*

Printed in Great Britain
by Amazon

33587010R00081